A DEREK DAX ADVENTURE
Second in a Series

CLASS PROPHECY: MURDER

A novel by **Dean F. V. Du Vall**

DAX ACTION BOOKS

FIRST EDITION

CLASS PROPHECY: MURDER Copyright ©1982 by Dean F. V. Du Vall. All rights reserved. Brief excerpts for review purposes permitted.

Published by:

DAX ACTION BOOKS
Division of Du Vall Press
Financial Publications
920 West Grand River
Williamston, Michigan 48895

DAX trademark reg. U.S. Pat. Off.

LIBRARY OF CONGRESS CATALOGING
IN PUBLICATION DATA

Du Vall, Dean F. V., 1940-

Class Prophecy: Murder!

I. Title. II. Series. III. Series: Derek Dax Adventure;2.
PS3554.U83C49 813'.54 80-65177
ISBN 0-931232-25-2 AACR2

Cover design by Hameed Noon

Printed in the United States of America

9 8 7 6 5 4 3 2 1

CLASS PROPHECY: MURDER

This book is dedicated to
YOU, if we met at the
enchanted cottage. Glad
you decided to pay a
return visit ...

1

Dear classmate,

Although it is certainly hard to believe a full two decades have gone by since together we all passed through the hallowed halls of good old Coolidge High, it is time for us to all get together once again for a fun-filled reunion!

I hope this mimeographed letter reached you all right. So many of us have moved away and gotten lost and I hate to be the one to tell you if you don't know but at least a half dozen or more of our number has dwindled due to death including Mark Packard, Johnny Arntz and Bob Ingles in Vietnam. But this letter is to announce a happy occasion — our 20th year class reunion!

The only problem is this; are there enough of us left who either care or can be found to make a such reunion possible? The last one, our fifteenth year, was not very well attended mostly because folks grumbled about having to travel so far just to get to our little old hometown which is not too exciting, I guess. There are only 4 of us out of the original class who still live in this area.

So I guess this is what I need to know. If you would come if we have one, would you think we should have it in some more glamorous place and would $15.00 for each registration (be sure to bring your husband or wife, too!) be a fair amount? That money would cover a dinner and a big meeting room I think.

Please let me know (if you get this letter!) what you think as soon as possible because it would be nice if we could plan the reunion for mid July or so to make it easy for those of you planning vacations.

(signed) Phyllis (Markum) Lindell, substitute class secretary*

*I am substitute because our beloved first one Mary Perkins killed herself 2 years ago.

Reading all that a second time, a bit more thoroughly once my interest was piqued by the signature, I mused silently, "Geez, no wonder editors go through life cranky, ulcerous and continuously on the offensive — if they are exposed to much of that sort of prose ..."

The letter had made a rather circuitous route over several of my temporary addresses before reaching me at my more or less permanent residence now nearing its total rebirth under the tender midwifery of my newly acquired confidante, one Kareem Khan.

I noted with amusement the stamp used to mail the letter. It was affixed upside down — the universal secret signal of 'I love you' used coyly by youngsters of another era. Nowadays, I'm sure teenagers are a bit more direct; "Yeah, Marge, we'll meet at Ralph's for a little dorking at midnight. I'll bring the shit — and you be sure to take a good dose of that damn Midol — I don't want no instant replay of your keepin' your pants on like last night ..."

Phyllis Markum! Good old Phyllis Markum! Good old hots-to-trots Phyllis — the gal who made our senior year class trip so memorable, as the other fellows and myself ganged together with eager Phyllis to test the sybaritic quality of the banks of the D.C. Tidal Basin long before old Wilbur and Fannie immortalized the site as the epitome of government excess gone mad.

My thoughts raced back to that period of the first half of my life. To the other 'kids' to use our euphemism of the day. I wondered how the others had faired thus far in their trek through life. How many were happily pursuing the original courses charted during that period in our history which, in retrospect seems so simple, comprehensible and even comfortable when seen in the harsh light of today's turbulent times.

Had Edgar Johnson in fact become a medical

doctor as he'd planned? Did Aloice Peterson actually try out for the space program as she seemed bent on doing? She always said she wanted to be the first woman in space, and those of us who thought she jested allowed as how if nothing else, she was one of the finer specimens of womanhood spaced out.

And Arthur Younger. I wonder if he actually became a mortician. The guy was our reigning class clown, yet for some reason ("Mon-ee!" he often volunteered as the motivation), he appeared really serious about joining that rather staid and stand-offish fraternity.

Of course, there was Jennifer Parker. But then I knew her story. We'd married three weeks after doffing our mortar boards, and ... Still, I hadn't had any contact with her in well over, what, eleven years? I wondered how she is getting along ...

"Phyllis? Phyllis Markum?"

"Yes, it's Phyllis ... Lindell, now. You must be one of our little flock of stray sheep checking in with the mama shepherd." She gushed in her same ridiculous way as always. "Just say a couple more words — I'll guess who you are."

"Well, let me see. Senior trip. Washington D.C. Tidal Basin. I was the one with the extra long ..."

"Oh, yes. Derek Dax. I recognize your voice, of course! Yes, you certainly *did* have exceptionally nice long ... eyelashes." She excused herself to tend a child howling in the background.

"My goodness, don't tell me you have a toddler, Phyllis! That's sort of late in life to be having babies, isn't it?"

"*Late?* That's my year-old *grandson* you hear there, I'll have you know!" Pride? Regret? Defensiveness? Hard to tell, as her voice just sounded exactly as it did twenty years ago — cheerful, hopeful and a bit too bubbly. "Derek, I am *really* glad that my letter found *you*! We've all been so pleased about your fantastic success as a writer! I always knew since right back there in Miss Whitehead's English class that you'd be a big famous writer someday!"

"Then yours was a cult of one, Phyllis! I always thought I'd be an internationally acclaimed motion picture star!"

"Well, maybe you will be yet! With a name like Derek Dax — say why'd you change your last name, anyway — oh, I know, all you big celebrities just thing it's 'real cool' to do that, isn't that right?"

"Well, not exactly ... it's a long story, and ..."

"Derek, I'm really sorry about your wife and daughter a couple years back — I couldn't believe it when I read that long list of victims on that terrible plane crash in Chicago ..."

"That's okay, Phyllis, I'm gradually getting over it, but listen, the reason I called, other than to hear your sparkling voice charm the phone lines, is to find out what the deal is on the reunion. Are you going to hold it or what?"

"Oh yes, it certainly looks like we'll have a splendid turnout for this one. The last, let's see, we've held three now — one every five years — haven't been too well-attended. The first, the five year one wasn't too bad, but ... say! YOU haven't come to any of them — why is that? We've missed you! Gotten too big for your old Hornet Hummer pals, huh?" She chided, but was still in good spirits. I had to think back to figure out the Hornet Hummer reference — the school's label for the football team.

"No, it's just that I've been busy and travelling a lot, and ..."

"No excuses or apologies necessary — just so you promise to come to this one!"

"Where is it being held, then?"

"Well now, that's the *real* problem! First, we had to make certain there'd be a decent turnout. We got over fifty of the guys and gals saying they'll come — most with their wives or husbands — but nobody can exactly agree on where to have it, except they sure as blue blazes don't want it in *this* little one-horse town. And frankly, I don't either, 'cause I'd like a real good excuse to get away from here myself for awhile. Got any ideas, Derek?"

I thought a moment, realizing the potential magnitude of my suggestion, but then thought what the hell ... "D.C. ... Washington. Or at least near there, in McLean, Virginia."

"Oh yeah? Why's that?"

"Well, you don't know it, because your letter to me was forwarded, and that reminds me, I'll have to give you my correct address ... But I have this huge estate here — about forty five acres or so with a big old three story mansion right in the middle. Has about forty two rooms as far as we can tell — every time we start at one end to count 'em, we lose track before we get to the other end." As I started to enthuse over the place, I felt increasingly boastful and tried to tone down my description a tad. "Anyway, it was a beat up old joint that we've been fixing up. Just about all done."

"We?" She inquired, obviously intrigued.

"Yah. A good friend. A great big devil of a fellow from Pakistan. You know, real dark brown, squeaky voice, and all that." I gave her my best impersonation of Kareem's distinctive contralto.

"Oh Derek, don't tell me that, like Chad, you've become a ..."

"Gay? To that, my dear, I can only refer your timeless memory back to that lofty Spring eve on the soft grassy knoll of ye olde Tidal Basin, and I assure you, that like a great vintage wine that gains its maximum potency and effectiveness only with the passing of time, I too, have improved commensurately through the years and need only your girlish charm to renew my passion ... Chad? Who's

Chad?" I interrupted my own soliloquy.

"You remember, Chad Carter. The tall thin fellow in biology with all the pimples? He called me just this morning. He's out in San Francisco. Driving a dairy truck I think he said. Anyway, he said he'd definitely come to wherever the reunion is held as long as everyone knows in advance that his companion, Robert somebody, is his lover. Can you believe that?"

"Oh yeah. Maybe he told you he drives a *fairy* truck, Phyllis, not a dairy truck. Also, when he leaves San Francisco, maybe he'll be leaving a part of his anatomy there other than his heart ..." I did an audio of a rim shot.

"What do you mean?" She said seriously.

Shit! It's no fun when they have to be explained. "His balls, Phyllis, his *balls!*"

"Oh Derek! Now, that's not nice."

I was getting a bit weary from all this, and beginning to regret my earlier suggestion that the reunion be held on my turf. But Phyllis had not forgotten. Maybe she takes notes.

"But Derek, why Washington for the reunion?"

Oh, why not. "Well, as I say, I have this great big place here, with a huge ballroom about the size of the gynmasium at Coolidge High, well not quite, but it is large, and I'd be glad to open the place for the reunion. There'd be plenty of room, and anybody bringing children could turn 'em out to pasture to keep them from underfoot.

"I'd furnish all the food and booze, of course, no one would have to pay for any of that — just their transportation and hotels — that sort of thing. You, of course, would be my personal guest at the mansion, since you are the pivotal person in this big bash. You and your husband, I mean.

"It would be a dandy way to inaugurate the old joint — it's over a hundred years old, and it's been essentially vacant for nearly twenty years. About time it saw some life, eh wot?"

"Why, I think it's a marvelous idea, Derek — and so generous of you, too! I just know that everyone will love the idea and they can even take side trips off to Washington and see the White House, the Lincoln Memorial, and ..."

"The Tidal Basin!" I twisted the memory again just for fun.

"Derek! That was a long time ago. Now, don't you go getting any ideas, again. I'm a happily married woman — a *grandmother*, remember." She was too emphatic for comfort. I've seen more than my share of pushing-forty, horny old out-of-shape babes, that come on to anything male that isn't in a wheelchair.

"Don't worry, I won't attack you in the middle of the night, Phyllis. I'll make sure you're assigned a room *without* a secret passage leading directly to my bedroom."

"Oh, well, you can put me in *that* room, if you like, just so *you* stay out of the passageway!"

I laughed, told her to check with the others, and firm up the details, and let me know. I told her the second or third weekend of July would be just fine for the event. Then, out of sheer deviltry I closed by asking, "Phyllis, my stamp was upside down. On the letter you sent me. I seem to remember that in our day that meant something special."

"Why yes, it did. It means 'I love you'."

"Did you put everybody's stamp on that way?"

"Oh no! But Chrissy — that's my thirteen year old — *she* did. She helped me prepare all the mail and she's at that syrupy, romantic age right now, so she stuck all the postage on upside down. She thought it a gesture of loving togetherness or something, I guess. Cute, yes?"

Yep. At least there's one adolescent out there emerging from puberty under the glare of blatant permissiveness with a bit of pureness and naivete. Maybe there's hope for us all yet.

2

I didn't mention the cottage to Phyllis. It still is, and will remain always a very private place for me. My refuge. To escape. To think. To write. And remember. Although the wiggling of that old sore tooth is less frantic, less insistent as it once was. As my best essay on the subject has already been executed, I would respectfully suggest that you peruse *"The Enchanted Cottage"* at your leisure, and thus become more fully apprised of its full meaning and impact, not just for me, but for yourself, as well.

That's where I was — at the cottage — doing a little skeletonizing of a forthcoming novel, when the phone rang — my only link to the outside world, with only one person privy to the number. I eased the receiver to my ear as I torched my pipe to life. "Yeah, Kareem. How's it going? Will they have that pool done on schedule?" I told him of the tentative plans for a reunion, and how the new swimming pool would come in handy to entertain folks, as would the regulation size tennis court which was already installed.

"Oh yes, it will be all finished by next week. That's why I bothered you, Mr. Dax. The landscape people are here, and that Mr. Lowe, the little arrogant pipsqueak guy, insists that you want the poodle bushes on the east side of the pool, but I was sure you specified the south."

I chuckled, knowing full well that the 'little pipsqueak' had to be standing nearby and was hearing the very apt description of himself, as Kareem would never speak in denigrating terms behind someone's back — not if they were still alive. "The south. You're right, Kareem, the poodles are to romp on the south side, okay? Anything else? No? Listen, I'll be up for dinner around six. You going to be there? Fine. See you then, and remember — Mr. Pipsqueak is a third your size, so don't sit on him too hard!" I heard his happy 'hee-hee-hee,' and the connection was severed.

I reflected upon my mental image of how the pool area and the surrounding gardens would appear when fully developed. I envisaged it precisely as Felicia had often described her dream of just such a project she planned to start at the home we shared as a family. It was her intention to begin the project immediately upon our return from the annual booksellers convention in Los Angeles, but that trip was never to be, due to that God-be-damned one ninety one — a foe who, whilst now held in abeyance, stood ever-ready to rear its ugly head once more.

The Japanese-styled garden with the pool constructed in a free-flowing style, fashioned to blend naturally rather than act as a garish focal point, would be my private memorium to my beloved Felicia and our daughter, Melissa. The garden would be a growing, thriving entity equal to the vibrancy of my departed loved ones.

Yes, this reunion idea was good. Being around young and alive people, old acquaintances and even a few good friends, as I recollect. Felicia would have been most supportive and taken full charge of all the preparations, which as I started to suddenly realize, would be monumental, to say the least. What did Phyllis say? Over fifty people plus their spouses? And probably scads of children ... uh oh ... what did I get myself into ...

★ ★ ★ ★

"Kareem, my friend, we have a problem."

"We do? I thought the project was going along fine. They'll be finished hanging the drapes tomorrow ..."

"No, no. The house is fine. The reunion, I mean. Do you realize we may be having between a hundred and fifty and two hundred guests in here for an entire weekend in a couple months?"

We had finished dinner and were having drinks in my new library, a magnificent room as it now stood nearly finished, yet one of the more unlikely choices for such a purpose when I first selected it. The area was massive, about the size of an average three bedroom tract house, with two grand columns imposing on the space, each situated about eight feet from either end of the shorter walls. A solid hand-hewn beam some twenty four inches square rested on the columns, thence running the full length of the room.

The beam was oiled and polished, and when we remodelled we needed only to clean it and apply varnish to restore its original lustre. Actually, the beam and the columns were the major design flaw of the entire mansion, which as a whole appeared to be designed almost as it was being built. That may be what attracted me to consider buying the place after the nefarious events which had brought it to my attention had passed.

I don't like every facet of life conveniently pigeon-holed. I detest labels. He's a writer. She's a nurse. They're Catholic. He's black. Life isn't all that neat and the things we do, are or expect, aren't that orderly or precise. So I liked the room, and the beam which looked so incongruous placed as it was the wrong way. We enjoyed an immediate ambience — me with my quirks, the room with its stupid-looking columns and mammoth beam up there in the sky.

The original panelling had years back been papered over for some unearthly reason by some flouncey female, no doubt — no man would ever cover up the beauty of natural wood like that, and if he did, he couldn't possibly select such a grotesque multi-colored floral pattern which, well, it defied and is not deserved of my description. When the wallpaper had been steamed away we polished the panelling for hours and hours, giving back its rightful soft-hued patina.

The mahogany floors were stripped, sanded and refinished. Floor to ceiling bookcases some fourteen feet high were built, utilizing the well-aged five-quarter poplar shelving that abounded in the basement. The fireplace, a truly handsome edifice created from Italian gold-veined black marble, was cleaned and allowed to reclaim its position as the room's dominant attraction — a command I'm certain it maintained when gentlemen and their ladies from another century wandered into its presence.

In addition to some fine overstuffed leather sofas and chairs, I installed a huge desk, some club chairs and a few other pieces.

"The place still looks empty. Needs something else important ..."

"It won't after your two hundred friends get

here. They'll fill it up."

"Yeah, see, now that's what I'm talking about — what are we going to do with all those people, huh?"

"I don't know. Was your idea, boss. But I think we'll manage it fine. I can get some help from the city. I'm certain Serenity would be happy to assist, too."

A brief pang of bittersweet zapped my sternum. "You haven't mentioned Serenity of late. Do you see her often? I miss her, myself."

"Oh, once in awhile I take her for a little spin in the Maserati. That's her favorite. Or we have a little dinner."

"You know you're welcome to bring her here — or anyone else, for that matter. When I asked you to come here and live, and said take over a whole floor for yourself, that's what I meant."

"Well, you know me — don't really need all that much breathing room like you do. My two rooms up there are just right for me. Don't you worry about me, Mr. Dax, I'm just fine."

"You do know though, we're going to have to get some live-in assistance to run this museum. A cook for sure — no reflection on that fabulous curry you make, but with my culinary expertise limited to a pretty decent charcoaled steak, and of course, my infamous 'Dax Breakfast Special,' plus your curry ... like I say, we need a cook. Also, we'll need some cleaning people, someone for yardwork ..."

"Don't worry — I'll take care of it. Really. That's the sort of thing I was good at when I was growing up in the palace. My father delegated that responsibility to me, overseeing the staff."

"I would think your father's boss, the Maharajah, from the way you've described him, would have thought you above all that. As well as he treated you, he might have sooner put his wife — what's she called, the Mahareenie — in charge of the domestic help."

"Are you kidding? She didn't do *anything* except keep the chief happy and spend all his rupees." Kareem began one of his fascinating dissertations about his life and times as a child when he lived in the palace of the Maharajah of Akhund in Pakistan, but was interrupted by the phone, which he answered. "Good evening. This is the residence of Mr. Derek Dax. This is Kareem Khan at your humble service."

I issued one of my clearly understood silent communications to Kareem, this one being, "Don't overdo it, Clyde — just say hello!"

"Yes, yes. This *is* Kareem Khan at your humble service."

My eyes lolled up into their sockets. If whoever was on the other end of the line only knew that their humble servant was a trained killer, trusted member of a super powerful and clandestine international organization dedicated to preserving

world order — at any cost — the caller would better
appreciate the humor at hearing my seven foot
friend speak so servilely with his high-pitched
delivery.

"Oh, thank you Mrs. Lindell. That is very nice.
Yes, yes. Mr. Dax is right here. One moment,
please." He handed me the phone, and in response to
my puzzled look prodded my memory. "Mrs.
Lindell. Your lady friend from the school reunion."

"Oh ... *Phyllis* ... I forgot her married name ..."

"Phyllis! That was quick. Don't tell me you got
ahold of everybody already. You did? But it's been
only a few hours since ... oh, a conference call — that
was very clever. What? No, Kareem is not a fag,
Phyllis, despite his funny little voice."

At hearing this, Kareem went into the funniest
damn swishy act I've ever seen in my life, and I
started to laugh. "Or maybe he is after all ... Most
everyone's excited about the idea, eh? Well, good.
Did you fix a date? Yeah, yeah. No, that's fine. The
second one. Okay ... no, no, I meant it, Phyllis. I think
it will be great. Did I tell you about the tennis court
and the new swimming pool? Oh yeah — first cabin
all the way.

"Well listen then, you go ahead now and change
his diapers and send me all the details when you and
... what's your husband's name ... Fred ... when you
two will be arriving, and we'll pick you up at the
airport. I would think, National. Well, whatever.

You let me know. Okay, goodnight, Phyllis." I sank
back in my chair, somewhat exhausted from the
conversation, but mostly from the realization that,
like it or not, we were going to be hosting a very
large and lengthy affair.

"Diapers? She changes her husband's diapers?"

"For all I know, perhaps she does, but in this
case she was referring to her grandson's diapers."

"Grandson ..."

"Why are you so wistful? Oh, I suppose out of
those six kids of yours you must have a grandchild
or two nipping about, eh wot? Do you ever see
them?"

"No." He declared flatly in his singular way that
closed the door to further discussion of the topic.

"A pool table!" I shouted, to change the mood.
"That's what we need in here. A great big old-
fashioned pool table! We'll get one. Also, I want to
set up a permanent floating chess game over there
somewhere. I've got several really nifty sets I've
collected over the years — been in storage too long.
We'll select an especially nice one and set it up.
Which reminds me, would you care for a match,
now?"

"No thank you, Mr. Dax. I've got a busy day
tomorrow, and better get to beddy-by. I've got to fly
to Bern and then onto Amsterdam. That's Q-T, by the
way."

"I thought your trip wasn't until next week."

"It wasn't, but that's part of the game. They spring little changes like that just to keep you on the toes."

"When you going to chuck all that stuff and concentrate on your painting?"

"Oh, I don't know. Sometimes I want to give it all up, just quit, but then something interesting comes my way, and I'm like that story of the old fire horse, still wanting to leave the pasture and get back in harness every time the bell rings ..."

"Yeah, me too. Every book I write is the last one until a fresh idea hits me, and I'm off and running — like you and that old fire horse. I'm working on a new novel right now."

"Well, good luck. Tell me about it sometime — maybe I can start getting a publicity hook for it."

"Okay, will do. Goodnight."

"Nighty-night."

3

As Kareem and I sat in the concourse awaiting the arrival of Phyllis Markum Lindell and her Fred, it occured to me that we had made no provision for recognizing one another, a foolish omission since a full twenty years had passed, and people do have a nasty habit of changing a tad in such a span, but then I figured the task of identification shouldn't be too difficult — just look for a fat and frumpy matron dragging some meek-looking bespectacled gent behind her.

But as the two hundred or so passengers made their way past us, I noted that we were starting to run out of likely candidates for players in my scenario. In fact, at last, all of our casting hopefuls had passed in review, and the flight attendants were now disembarking, no doubt anticipating a fun-filled layover in the nation's capitol.

"Are you sure that was two-twenty-four, Kareem? I don't see anyone who ..."

"Derek! Derek Dax, there you are?" I turned to

see two women jostling back through the straggling remnants of passengers, and sure enough, one was obese and disheveled, my solitary vision of what grand ma-ma Phyllis had surely become after the rigors of time and circumstances. Strange though, she wasn't the one hollering my name. It was a younger, much thinner lady, rather stunning in appearance I noted, and as she neared she grabbed me in a passionate bear hug.

"Derek, you devil! You let us prance right past you ..."

"Phyllis? Why it is you, isn't it ... why you're beautiful!"

"Well, of course! What'd you expect, a dowdy old broad with a sack full of home baked cookies? Just because I'm a grandmother doesn't mean I'm *dead!*"

Then began the first of what over the next couple days was to become a common, albeit treacherous little game played out at all such reunions, I imagine — trying to guess with only minimal cobwebbed clues the identity of some erstwhile classmate as thrust in your presence by some other childhood friend already in the know.

"Come on now, Derek — you remember this girl — she was in our home room — sat right behind you — had a big crush on you ..."

I looked at the pudgey little face and saw embarrassment, self consciousness and fright, and then remembered. "Carlita! Carlita Phillips! But of course I remember you." And I kissed her on the lips, purposely lingering a moment too long — in slight retribution for my sins of youth which included too frequent and hurtful remarks about the girl's obesity.

Introductions were made all around, Kareem easily toted the women's luggage by himself, waving off the offered assistance of myself and a nearby redcap. Phyllis explained that her Fred hadn't really wanted to make the trip, and since Carlita would have been by herself, she decided to ask her along. She hoped it was all okay with me, and I assured her that indeed it was, that I was just glad they were both able to arrive today, so we could discuss final preparations before the arrival of the full influx of guests expected Saturday morning.

The ladies, especially Phyllis, were duly impressed with our conveyance, the chauffeured Cadillac limosine belonging to Kareem's publicity agency, and the ride to the estate was appropriately filled with 'ohs and ahs' and other delighted mutterings of two small-town inhabitants un-leashed in the big time. I remembered the feeling quite vividly, myself.

At one point during the journey, when the buzzer announced existence of the on-board tele-phone, Phyllis enthused, "Why, you live just like royalty, Derek — what a far cry from your humble beginnings."

I thought I sensed a tinge of jealousy — even resentment, but decided I was over-reacting. I resolved to relax and let my success be shared openly, and without question — especially by little Carlita, who despite her excess weight seemed small and vulnerable. I reasoned that this might be her one big escapade in life, and decided to help her make the most of it.

"What do you like to do most, Carlita? Swim? Play tennis? Ride horses? Stroll through the meadows? We've got quite a list of goodies to choose from out here." We were just entering the main gate, the long-winding, shrub-lined road leading to the mansion lay before us. I felt a strong sense of pride as the limo silently floated along the path. For a fact, as Phyllis had previously and a bit tersely reminded me, I had indeed come a very long way since last we met, and I make apologies to no one for that fact. It had been a long, hard, often bitter trip that now brought me, us, to this pleasant station in life.

"Oh, it's just lovely, Derek. So peaceful and calm. You must be truly happy here."

I smiled at Carlita, and reminded her that she hadn't told me of her favorite sport or pastime.

"Oh, just *being* is sometimes all I care to do."

I glanced at Phyllis who was making a gesture that said, "And stuff herself with food." I frowned at her, and got in return another visual message.

"Well, it's true!"

At the mansion, further introductions were made. Serenity had driven out earlier, insisting on helping with overseeing the weekend catering chores, and a half dozen domestics were brought in and given to understand that essentially, Phyllis would be in command of their forces, since in reality she was running the whole show.

Kareem carted everyone's luggage off to the upper levels, and I showed the women their rooms, reassuring Phyllis that my room was just three doors down, but indeed did not have a secret passageway to her chambers. She expressed coquettish regret, and Carlita, herself an accomplished silent mugger, shot me an, "Oh brother!" look, and the ladies went off to do whatever it is ladies do when they breezily advise us hairy ones that they'll just be a minute or so freshening up.

Over dinner we discussed the upcoming itinerary, the list of confirmed guests, and a smaller number of hope-to-but-not-sure-yets, plus we talked of the old days at Coolidge High. We finally admitted in joyful conspiracy that those days were not really all that grand and glorious, after all.

Carlita dragged out her four high school year books, and we marveled at all the crazy things everybody had written, the funny-looking pictures of us all, and Serenity remarked with mild surprise that only two black students appeared anywhere in the pages.

"That's because there were only two nigger families allowed in the entire town, dear." And then Phyllis paled, as she closely scrutinized Serenity's finely negroid features, "Oh, I didn't realize you're ..."

"Black? Well, I'm not black in color — just in race."

"She is a child of the world." That was Kareem, with his doting, faraway voice inflection. Serenity, true to her name, is the only person who has a noticeable calming influence on the Pakistani fireball.

At eleven, Phyllis announced it was bedtime for her, and Carlita agreed, so the little group disbanded for the night. Kareem disappeared, and Serenity and I lingered for one last drink.

"I hope you didn't take offense at Phyllis' off-handed remark. You must realize that she ..."

"Oh, you know better than that, Derek. I've been through all the outright attacks of prejudice, as well as the sneaky little innuendos from real pros. She's harmless. But she does have her bedroom eyes on you, but then I'm sure you're aware of that."

"No, I don't think so. Besides, I'm saving myself for you, dear." I'd said it lightly, but our eyes met briefly, causing a serious exchange.

"But you know that's not possible."

"I know, but ..." My voice trailed off as she

kissed me affectionately on the forehead, patted my cheek and said, "Goodnight."

"Goodnight, Serenity ..." God I loved that woman, but in a strange spiritual way, similar, I guessed, to that of her most ardent admirer, Kareem, who loved her from afar, with more respect and awe than simple raw passion.

I had just dozed off when a noise awakened me, and I heard the rustle of someone approaching the bed. No one spoke, and soon the lithe naked figure that lay down beside me in the dark, urged both of us to a passionate fulfillment. She never said a word. Nor did I. At dawn, I awoke ... alone.

At the breakfast table I looked from Serenity's dark piercing eyes to the gray vacuous ones of Phyllis — but got no clue.

Kareem's ever-present sixth sense or 'sick sense' as he pronounces it, caught something inordinate in the air, but later when he asked, "What was going on at breakfast?" I could only reply, "You really wouldn't believe it if I told you."

But it was true. One of those ladies had come to me in the midst of slumber, offered herself to me in total abandon, then slipped away without identifying herself. Or did I dream it ...

4

It took a convoy consisting of several taxies, a liveried bus, the limosine plus a few of my personal cars driven by Serenity, Kareem and myself to get the gang from the airport and bus terminal to the estate, but by noon Saturday most everyone was gathered and happily renewing the acquaintance of long-lost souls in the sea of progressive change.

I had personally escorted two couples in the Silver Wraith, one consisting of a scrawny birdlike female I remembered only as being a withdrawn, quiet sort who now, seized upon every possible opportunity to berate each action of her teddy bear type husband, who passively sat allowing her barbs to flick off his padded exterior.

The other couple was headed by Paul Arbaugh, a serious straight laced fellow who in school always copped any awards for scholastic achievement. He now appeared to be genuinely discomfited by such a flight of fancy as attending a twenty year class reunion, and mentioned that, like myself, he'd never

taken the time to attend any previous such gather-
ings. But he added wistfully, "Life is short, and this
may very well be the last chance we all have to see
each other." But his voice clearly telegraphed that
he didn't give a damn if that happened or not.

Arbaugh's wife was a striking, almost awesome
appearing woman some ten years his junior. She
was reserved, but wholly sophisticated, truly
aristocratic in her carriage. Her expensively
tailored suit belied what my on-the-fritz x-ray
vision told me was an exquisitely perfect female
figure. Long legs, slim waist, slightly enlarged
hips, medium bosom, and long white neck.

Her tapered fingers and meticulous manicure
bespoke the fact of pampered indulgence. Her name
was Lydia. Why not — it fit her image, if not her
youth.

My idle inquiry as to the occupation or
profession of the two gentlemen brought a "Plumb-
ber — goin' on twenty-five years," from the teddy
bear, but from Paul Arbaugh only a vague response
of, "Research, mostly. Some creative science." His
tone indicated that he'd rather not talk about it as I
was probably too dumb to understand anyway, so I
didn't press.

We soon joined the others, arriving from
original embarkments from twenty nine states and
two foreign countries, including a totally bald
fellow from Saudi Arabia whom I could not

remember at all, even after studying his pictured name tag which displayed a full shock of hair and the name Clarence Hildahl.

As the people started to mill about, the gregarious, the timid, the instantly recognizable either through the good graces of gentle aging, or from cartoon-like caricatures of their original selves, I stepped to the p.a. system and officially welcomed one and all. I told them to feel right at home, to enjoy all the amenities of the estate, and asked them only to please not pee in the pool or do anything perverted on the beds without first turning down the covers, and then turned the microphone over to Phyllis, "Our respected mother shepherd," who received an enthusiastic ovation for her "fine and untiring devotion to rounding up her far-flung flock and bringing us together for at least one more frolic."

Phyllis gushed her official welcome to the assemblage, read off a detailed schedule of what we were all going to be doing for the next couple days, and when we were expected to do it. She directed everyone's attention to a bulletin board to which were pinned cards and letters of regrets from those unable to attend. Everyone was urged to have a real fun time and to make use of the estate's facilities as "graciously provided by our most successful classmate, Derek," and in closing she directed everyone to the cafeteria-style counters, heaped with varied and delicious foods kept replenished by the ever-alert catering staff which flitted about for the duration.

As the day progressed, I noted that Kareem's specially prepared curry was the star attraction, as was the man himself, delighting all, but especially the children with his tales of life in the palace.

The afternoon's festivities were bright and gay, with everyone seeming to have a genuinely terrific time of it. Several couples put the tennis court to good use, others drifted off to explore the grounds on our six Apaloosas, but most just lounged in and around the pool, reviving old memories. Only a few guests had brought children, and most of them spent hours in the pool or roaming the wooded areas of the estate.

"It's a great place for kids, Derek. Not quite like the bleak coal bins and railroad tracks of our day." It was Paul Arbaugh, come to join me on the deck overlooking the pool, possibly I suspicioned, to keep a watchful eye on me, since I was rather obtrusively keeping both of mine on his wife, Lydia, who was amongst the few women brave enough to bikini her way into the pool.

I didn't reply to his comment which was more of a statement of fact than a question. "Your wife is extraordinarily beautiful, Paul. You're a very lucky man. How did a staid old bookworm like you land such a beauty?"

"Well, even bookworms go fishing now and again, and one day I must have cast my pole in just the right pond."

I looked at him and chuckled appreciatively, acknowledging the surprisingly clever retort from an otherwise serious and totally humorless man.

"She's younger than I. Was my research assistant at Tech. We just worked well together, and made it a permanent arrangement, I guess."

"Does she still work with you, now?"

"Not as much anymore. We adopted a child two years ago, and he takes up most of her time. He's six, now."

We talked a bit longer, and I started to say something, but as if reading my thoughts, Arbaugh said, "Don't concern yourself with an apology, Derek — about those somewhat lascivious thoughts regarding Lydia. It's natural. I don't blame you, in fact, I get sort of a strange charge from watching other men drool over her, do you understand?"

I smiled. "Remember how I gloated over the nice comments you made about my Silver Wraith earlier whilst we were driving in ...?"

He smiled, and made it clear that we were on the same wave length. As he walked away, I thought how odd it was that out of all the kids I grew up with, Paul Arbaugh should now, twenty years later, turn out to be the one with the most promise as a simple, honest human being. No axes to grind, no glad-

handing, brown-nosing or displays of bravado like
so many of the others.

No wonder the bookworm had baited and landed
such a graceful catch. Like Starkist's Charlie, Lydia
Arbaugh had good taste.

The afternoon passed quickly, with several of
the guests producing copies of my various books
and insisting upon all sorts of intimate, personal
inscriptions. I obliged. You takes your thrills
wherever and whenever you find them.

At four o'clock, Kareem delivered unto us a late
comer, one Janine Taylor, an erstwhile heart-
breaker of the entire group of senior class males,
although she had gotten to my glands long before
that. After she'd made the rounds, I singled her out
and reminded her of that fact. "You probably didn't
know or care for that matter, but back in sixth grade
— Miss Willis's class — remember, the old gal with
the permanently fixed right index finger, plus a
crotchety stare to match — well, on Valentine's Day,
my birthday, you came to school wearing a bright
red and white-laced frock, and I must tell you, you
all but tore my heart out! You were a vision of
lovliness."

I then went on to ask if she remembered
receiving an anonymous note in the mail, implor-
ing her to meet her secret admirer at a certain
section in the basement of Carnegie Public Library,
and whether she remembered her mother in fact,

driving her there in a polished green Chevrolet sedan — because I certainly recalled every part of the dreamlike sequence, since although I was too shy back then to make myself known as the guilty instigator of the aborted affair, I did lie in the bushes adjacent to the library and anxiously peer into the basement window at the singular object of my affections as she impatiently paced the designated section which contained a small collection of love sonnets.

But no, she now claimed no recollection of the incident whatsoever, nor thought it especially signifiant or even amusing that I now revealed the truth of my childhood passion for her. Indeed, she appeared totally uninterested and preoccupied, and excused herself to go talk to a much out of shape rotunda, once the revered jock of the Hornet Hummers.

"Bitch!" I muttered, not too quietly under my breath as she flounced away. Perhaps I should have told her that even now, lo these twenty five years after my maddening sixth grade crush, she still had the power to stir passion in my loins — but the fact is, she did not. Whereas once, she was fresh, beautiful, albeit a cock-teaser, to use the vernacular of the day — now she was but a used-up, worn-out version, too tanned, too lined — a terrible mockery of what once was.

"Yes, she is a bitch — but she's still a hell of a

good lay!" Someone had approached me from behind, and heard my not well concealed parting remark to Janine. I whirled around to see Alan Wilson, who appeared exactly as if he'd stepped from the Hornet Hummer yearbook and onto my patio without suffering one iota the ravages of time. I told him so.

"Well, I keep in shape. Plus, a face lift every now and then keeps it looking fairly tight."

He was himself a plastic surgeon, lived in Malibu, and indicated that he enjoyed a most successful practice. It had been Alan, who when we were about nine or ten, collaborated with me on my first attempt at novelizing. It was called, *"The Wilson Twins Mystery,"* and we had had great fun devising what we thought was a grand plot.

"I'm glad to see one of us made it, Derek — as a writer, I mean. I have no regrets for myself, God knows, but every now and then, especially when I'm writing a paper for the Journal or something, I get that little nostalgic sense of what it might have been like — the wild and abandoned life of a famous writer — living freely in the wilds of Virginia." He waved his arms, encompassing the reaches of my estate.

"Well, that's why you're a doctor, Alan — and I'm a writer — your prose stinks! Living freely in the wilds of Virginia ... Geez!"

We laughed and he oh-by-the-way asked

me to not mention his comment about Janine being a
good lay to his wife, Miriam. "California's a
community property state, you know — I'd hate to
have to cut my new Mercedes in half." He laughed
nervously, but I assured him that his secret was safe
with me, and I pointedly suggested that he, himself
keep his stupid mouth shut about Janine, because I
couldn't vouch for anyone else's discretion but my
own.

During the course of the day enough of my old
chums had asked me why I'd changed my last name,
so by the time Rosemary Cadley posed the question,
my answer was routine. "Well, when I first started
writing, it was during a time when the show biz
folks were very big on coming up with clever new
names for actors, actresses and a number of writers
as well thought it the in-thing to do.

"My old name, Daceskny, sounded like something unspeakable a back alley doctor might do to
you for an exhorbitant fee, so I shortened it — before
the doctor could get a chance to do it." (That
generally evokes a ribald snicker or two.) "At first, I
spelled it D-a-c-s, but noticed people pronounced it
Dakes — with a long a — so then, I just simplified it
to Dax, although now some people, who only see the
name in print, will pronounce it Docs, rather than
rhyming it with axe. Can't win 'em all, as my friend,
Kareem, is fond of saying."

Just then, a contingent of sight-seers returned

from a visit to some of Washington's historical exhibits and regaled the others with exciting descriptions of the marbelized, pigeon-dropping repositories.

Towards dusk, we mostly broke up the group, to rest, refuel and refresh for the evening's festivities which were to include dinner, some dancing to music of the Beatle era, plus the piece de resistance — the reading of the class will and prophecy, a once cherished, but now mostly forgotten document executed shortly before graduation, and then stored in the vault of Ernie Tucker's father's bank.

No one seemed to be able to recall a word of what they had personally committed to the mini time capsule which was soon to be made public for the first time. I certainly did not remember anything about it. But evidently someone surely did, and that fact was to have onerous impact on the balance of our happy little reunion.

5

Arthur Younger, 'Artie' as he insisted everyone call him, was, as far as I could ascertain, the only member of our conclave to have actually pursued and succeeded at his original calling, which in his case resulted in him now owning one of the largest chains of funeral parlors in the country. At one point earlier in the day, he and Victor Louden, a little runt of a fellow who never seemed to grow either in mind or stature, did their best to outdo each other with gruesome tales, real or imagined events each had experienced with the dead or dying — Artie at his mortuary, and Victor on his ambulance calls in New York City.

Kareem overheard part of their conversation, and interrupted them long enough to relate a particularly grisly reminiscence of his own, and shortly thereafter, I noticed Victor heading for a wooded area, and Artie pulling hard at a tall drink.

"What the hell did you say to those guys to send Victor off to puke up my woods, and old Artie there to suddenly become an alcoholic?"

"Oh, nothing much. Just how, during the war one day I returned from a low strafing mission, and wondered why my craft was running sort of rough. When I got out I smelled some meat burning, and looked in the front scoop and found the top half of..."

"Never mind!"

"You *asked*..." He said wickedly.

Artie had managed to retain his singular sense of humor, despite his profession, and it was an unspoken codicil that our old class clown would act as master of ceremonies for the evening's main event in the ballroom. He dutifully kicked off the affair with a rather touching eulogy for those of our original class who had, by accident or design, passed on to a greater reward a tad early, including the fellows who had given their all in Viet Nam, and a married couple, sweethearts since kindergarten, who, with their infant son had perished in a fire two years after graduation, plus,

"...of course, our original class secretary, Mary Perkins, who served us so well and too often, thanklessly — in fact, maybe that's why she did herself in..."

"Gross, Artie, gross! You know she had cancer!" Someone shouted from the center of the crowd.

"Yeah, I'm sorry, folks. Not all of 'em are gems.. but here are a couple that are ..." And he launched into a brief monology of fairly crisp and current one-liners.

Then, he officially introduced Phyllis to the assemblage, said a few nice and a few raunchy things about her, and presented her with fat bouquet of red roses declaring the combined expression of love and appreciation for all of us.

This was followed by a voice vote on who should be declared the most versatile and accomplished amongst us, and after a couple flattering suggestions that the award be given to the weekend host, I arose and respectfully demurred, stating that obviously we had a fait accompli before us in fellow classmate, Myron Jenkins, who had two decades before been my locker mate in gym, but now, as best I could determine from my earlier observation at poolside, had bested us all by the superior accomplishment of becoming a highly desirable and attractive *Myra* Jenkins.

Enthusiastic applause followed my nomination, and Myra, one very luscious lady indeed, graciously accepted the little trophy which had a gold plastic figure of a hornet on top.

Clarence Hildahl won hands down the award for having travelled the farthest, from Saudi Arabia, over Peggy Winslow who had journied from Calgary, Alberta, Canada.

Finally, we got to what had become a highly anticipated climax, as during the past few hours everyone seemed to be preoccupied with the contents of the wax-sealed envelope containing our individual and collective hopes for the future — a prophecy made in another time, in the bright light of hope, promise and naivete. It did portend a chuckle or two, plus a sense of nostalgia, and with the others I eagerly looked forward to the unveiling.

"For all these many years," Artie intoned as dramatically as possible, "Our trusted classmate — and who could be more trusted than a banker — Ernie Tucker, has carefully guarded our treasure with his very life, and now, folks, it is time to bust its cherry and see what exciting promises come forth!"

"Gross, Artie — gross as hell — there are *ladies* present!"

Everyone laughed, and Artie introduced Ernie Tucker.

"Like Artie said, I have kept this parcel under my auspices for quite a long time now, and I'm sort of glad to finally be able to relinquish my responsibility. Just to refresh your memory, originally we put this in a safety deposit box at dad's bank, and then, after the explosion and fire. . ." Tucker hesitated, obviously reliving a painful experience, ". . . and dad's death. . . I kept the thing at home for awhile until the new bank was built. But I assure you I never peeked inside it, despite the fact it was scorched and the seal was melted free." The crowd chuckled at that. "Then, after the new bank was built, and since then, as president of the bank..."

A note of pride had crept into his voice and was quickly replaced by a strain of levity, as he concluded with, ". . . and until now, it has been hermetically sealed in a mayonaise jar, and since noon yesterday kept on the porch of Funk and Wagnalls. . ."

The group applauded good naturedly, and he turned over the document package to Phyllis, who began by dolefully reminding us that our class president was Bob Ingles, one of the trio killed in the war, so she guessed if it was okay with everybody, she would do the honors. A round of applause urged her on and she began.

First, there was an upbeat general class prophecy written by two girls from the Quill and Scroll Society. It was in the form of a letter to Mr. Penske, our D.C. trip benefactor, and the man to whom our senior yearbook was dedicated. The letter was ostensibly written twenty years in the future, now in fact, and told of colonies on the moon and Mars, and somehow managed to weave into the tale's fabric a word or two about each of our individual hypothetical exploits.

The letter droned on, and at last mercifully concluded with, "The next morning, after our interesting and enjoyable trip, we returned to the Rocket Port and boarded our ship for home. We hope you have enjoyed our letter as much as we have enjoyed writing it to you, Mr. Penske. Yours truly,

Becky Sue and Constance."

The two writers of the epistle were now present, and rose to acknowledge the polite applause for their effort. One lady seated across the table from me mentioned that it was too bad that Mr. Penske wasn't still alive to enjoy the moment, and her companion suggested that "At least he went out with a real bang — even better than that hokey rocket trip." His reference was to the fact the Penske had shocked everybody by marrying one of our classmates shortly after graduation, and had then suffered a fatal cerebral hemorrhage during the honeymoon.

Next came the class will, preceded by a short paragraph which traditionally attested to our being of a collective sound and disposing mind and memory, and bequeathing through our last will and testament various cute and sophomoric items such as;

"I, Max Andrews, leave to Victor Luden, who needs it more than anyone I know, my six foot two inches."

"To Angie King, I leave Ervin Kueschal, now that I'm done with him."

The Pasquale twins bequeathed "All our matched sets of clothes to Merry and Gerry — except our sequinned prom gowns which we plan to wear in heaven."

And my own, "To any insecure sap who wants it,

my superior wit and inflated ego with this reminder, I don't think I'm so great, but what's my humble opinion compared to millions of others?"

There were titters from the crowd after most of the inane declarations, and finally we got to the part everyone anticipated, the reading of individual carefully recorded hopes and dreams for our personal futures.

A hushed silence pervaded the room, although a few murmers along the lines of "This should be good!" could be heard.

The prophecy was actually a collection of individully prepared sheets, each containing the handwritten or typed insight of a class member. Phyllis began her reading logically, in alphabetical order, and if the class member was present, he or she would join her and stand patiently as the haunting words were read aloud.

As Phyllis read off the statements one could feel a peculiar sense of de' ja vu building in the room as yet another of us heard our private thoughts of long ago jogging our memory laconically or loquaciosly depending upon the mood and sense of posterity at the time of writing.

There were a few, who upon hearing their one-time dreams revealed publicly — dreams which had not been fulfilled — broke down and wept. Others laughed off their once youthful aspiration and predictions, and a couple reacted only by ceremoniously lifting a glass.

Artie, ever adept at maintaining a festive mood, took the mike for a spate, cracked a joke about our group being deader than an undertaker's convention, and suggested that the next prophecy ought to be on the brighter side, since it was "... none other than that of our congenial and jovial host, Derek Dax."

There was an enthusiastic round of applause, more from a collective desire to break the mounting tension than anything, and Phyllis stepped back to the microphone just as the applause faded and a piercing soul-wrenching scream destroyed the weekend.

6

The scream, a distinctly feminine screech, came from Chad Carter, our fairy fine fellow who had evidently left the ball room after hearing his prophecy revealed, for he now was running into the room from the general vicinity of the garden.

"Please help! There's a *body* out there! He's dead, oh, I just know he is *dead!*" And then he promptly fainted in the arms of Robert, who had run to greet his lover at the first sound of his voice.

The crowd stood stunned for a second, then, as one, started running towards the garden. I was still on the platform where I'd gone when I knew my prophecy was up next. As the area cleared, I noted from the corner of my eye a brown hand dart out and gather up the prophecy parcel.

It didn't take long to discover the source of Chad's anguish, as those to reach the area first were shouting the news. "There's a body in the pool!" "Who is it?" "Are you sure he's dead?" "What happened?"

It was Paul Arbaugh, lying face down in the center of one of the smaller reflecting pools, a design feature Felicia had considered just the right touch of superlative decadence in her overall design of the gardens. Three or four of the men jumped into the pool and started to haul out the body, but they were stopped by a high-pitched command from Kareem, "Stop! Don't move!"

They looked up in time to have their surprised expressions forever encapsulated in celluloid as Kareem clicked away furiously with his Nikon.

"Is that enough, pal? Can we see if he's dead, now?" It was Alan Wilson, standing knee-deep in water who now directed his assistants in the removal of Arbaugh to the grassy surface adjacent to the pool. Hurriedly, Wilson started manual resuscitation efforts, but he stopped when Kareem stepped next to the body, pushed Wilson aside and deftly flipped the body over to reveal a small stiletto protruding at a sickening angle from Arbaugh's chest.

A gasp arose from the crowd and women turned their heads aside.

Kareem solomnly said, almost to himself, "Too much water is not his problem, doctor, but too little blood ..."

In the two years since my first meeting Kareem, then known only to me as my publicity agent, hired by my publisher for the eastern tour of my latest book release, I'd grown to respect the man immensely. His intellect, his insight and even his compassion are revealed in extraordinary ways at the most peculiar times. Often we had discussed his 'other' job, though mostly in the abstract, as he seldom discusses, even with me, any of the details of his assignments.

But one of our oft repeated discussions had centered on the intricasies and idosyncrasies of crowd psychology. He had apparently been 'on location,' as he calls it, during a number of coups in more than a few nameless third world countries.

His description of how a crowd tends to take on the personality of its most dominant member, and how it is extremely difficult for even an impartial bystander to avoid being drawn into the fray, even if the purpose or ideology of the crowd is totally contrary to one's own — all that utterly fascinated me

I had likened the phenomena to that of one's trying to act against the pervasive crowd psychology in the stock market — something I had prided myself on being able to do each time I dabbled — rather profitably, I might add.

So it was then, with the scene before me — of men and women hovering about, consoling one another, and issuing exclamations of grief, wonderment and excitement at the grisly scene layed out before them — that I tried to mentally remove myself from the mild hysteria of the others, and observe the actions of as many of the party as possible.

I recorded a dozen or so of the more interesting and unusual of these in my little mental file, the one nearly as calibrated and retrievable as a Roledex.

Wilson semi-officially pronounced Arbaugh quite dead, and the crowd, as if before having doubts of this, murmered their acknowledgement. Several of those nearest the scene started to leave — there not being much else to do, but Kareem stood up, his massive frame compensating in authority for the tiny voice which announced, "There has evidently been a murder here. We shall, of course, contact the authorities. No one must leave the premises, although you are free to leave this immediate area and go back to the ballroom or elsewhere."

Several suggestions of "Let's go get a drink" were interrupted by a lonely voice that asked, "But where is Mrs. Arbaugh?"

Again, the interesting reaction of the crowd, as each member turned to his or her neighbor — even a wife or husband — to see if somehow they had been miraculously supplanted by the personage of Lydia Arbaugh.

But she was not to be found — at least in this vicinity.

Amongst cries that, "Someone must find her — tell her!" the crowd, now instilled with fresh purpose — something to do — started to fan out in search of the new widow, each bent on being the privileged one to break the ghastly news.

If I sound sardonic, then perhaps I am, but truthfully I report only the facts and fallacies of the human animal reacting under stressful and unique circumstances. Some laugh uncontrollably at funerals whilst, as well-known, others sob at weddings.

A few will go to their death willingly, even eagerly, but others of us cling beyond all reasonable hope to the precious thread that connects us to the reality of life.

So, we're a weird lot in many respects, but upon close examination, our varied reactions and actions can generally be explained, if not fully understood.

Perhaps, the foregoing will also help to explain my own reaction following the pool discovery, which was a desire to get away from it all, especially the people milling about — as soon as possible. I tend to get claustrophobic and agitated when thrust into even a normal crowd situation, and frequently, to compensate, I will launch into some ridiculous routine to draw attention to myself, when in reality I'd rather folks ignore me. I'm very popular at the few parties I attend.

But given the totally abnormal vibrations of this group, which boarded on the hysterical, my impulse was to remove myself. And so I did.

As I walked alone in the darkness I mulled over as many of the smaller scenes I'd mentally recorded as well as the larger vignette, itself. Something was out of place, didn't jive with the rest of the picture, but I couldn't put my mind on it directly, so just continued reviewing all the things that were still clear.

Before long I was at the cottage. No doubt that's where I had in mind going when I left the pool area, although I'd made no conscious decision to head in that direction. The lights were out, of course, and as had become my custom of leaving it so, the door was unlocked. I didn't want to risk being disturbed, so I left the place in darkness and went into the great room.

I sank into the couch and lighted my pipe, taking great and thoughtful drags. The final one caused the flame to shoot up several inches illuminating the immediate space surrounding me, and I noted a figure reposing in the wing-back next to the hearth.

Not knowing if perhaps it was another body to worry about, I approached the figure gingerly, using my lighter as a torch. I saw at once it was a woman and shook her shoulders gently. She sprang to life instantly, and sat bolt upright. "Whaat? Who? What is it? Paul?"

"No, Mrs. Arbaugh, it's Derek. Are you all right?"

"Yes. Oh, Mr. Dax, it's you."

I fumbled for the switch on a small table lamp. "Please call me Derek, Mrs. Arbaugh."

She laughed, "That's rather silly. I call you Derek, and you call me Mrs. Arbaugh?"

"Well, we have now settled that problem, *Lydia.*" I remained silent then, feeling very awkward. If Lydia Arbaugh had killed her husband, then it was pointless of me to tell her he was dead. If she hadn't, then I was about to cop the big prize all my aging classmates and their spouses were running around the mansion trying to claim; I would be the one to break the news. The prospect of that was not appealing. I sat numbly for a moment, choosing my words.

"You really loved her, didn't you. And still do."

I had trouble adjusting to the change of focus. "Beg pardon? Loved who, my wife?"

"Oh yes, certainly. But I had reference to Penelope Goodbody. You loved her in an extraordinary, timeless way — the way I loved Paul."

"You knew Penelope? But how is that possible?"

She smiled, a secretive little movement of her mouth, as one conspirator to another, and tapped a long fingernailed index on a copy of *"The Enchanted Cottage"* which rested on the end table next to the chair.

"Is it any good?" I inquired a bit testily. "A few copies just arrived yesterday morning, but I haven't really had a chance myself to read the final form."

"Oh, it's marvelous, and having read your book and learned about this extraordinary cottage, I don't feel it necessary to apologize for intruding here without asking for permission. In fact, I felt the enchantment of the place the moment I entered — even before I discovered the book here. It sort of embraces and protects, doesn't it ..."

I didn't want to ask, or tell, or do anything to destroy her few remaining minutes of sanity and personal life orderliness, so I just sat and puffed my briar, trying not to be too obvious as I gazed at her truly beautiful face. My grandmother had collected porcelain dolls and the unspoiled perfection of this lady's face reminded me of just such a doll, except she had warmth, and ..."

"He's dead, isn't he. Paul. He's dead." She didn't look up, and hers was not a question, but an affirmation of fact.

"You know? But how? Surely you didn't ..." Some detective I am — I'm telling the prime suspect she didn't commit the crime.

"Kill him? Yes and no. No, in the sense that I didn't shoot him or whatever it is they did to him. But yes, in that I knew ... *he* knew ... that it would happen, but I allowed him to convince me we were powerless to do anything to stop it. But I couldn't believe that, and I implored him to let me go to the authorities, and try to get protection. But he said it would only make matters worse for me and Daniel, our son ... afterwards. So I did not follow my instincts, and did nothing to prevent ..." She allowed her voice to trail off.

I sat listening to all this in pure bewilderment. My pipe had burned down, and I tapped the ashes out, refilled it, slowly got it burning again — taking as much time as possible to avoid saying, "I'm really sorry, Mrs.Ar..., Lydia, but I cannot understand any of that story. And I'm afraid the police aren't going to either. Perhaps we'd best go on back to the main house ..."

"But of course you can't or won't believe it!" She was beginning to sound a bit hostile, and like any caged animal intent on self-preservation I looked around for a quick escape, or a possible weapon in case she produced one of her own. "And if you won't believe it, his own friend and classmate, how could perfect strangers be expected to believe it?"

I started to say something about Paul and I being only one-time buddies during our eighth grade coal bin and railroad track days, but was interrupted by a quick knock on the door. Seeing who it was, I shouted gratefully, "Come in, Kareem."

He politely acknowledged Mrs. Arbaugh's presence, as though he'd known she would be there all along, and to me, "Mr. Dax, I think both of you should come to the house. The police are there, and ..." He looked at me for a sign that Mrs. Arbaugh knew of her husband's death, and when I nodded, he concluded, "... and there has been another murder."

Lydia Arbaugh rushed to my side, and held my arm, but her real mission was that of surreptitiously pressing a folded paper to my hand.

"It's okay, Lydia, Kareem is on your side if you deserve it." Quickly, I read the note, and shoved it in my pocket, had second thoughts, and handed it to Kareem. Unless someone were aware of his glass jaw on which one light tap will send him sprawling unconscious, they'd think twice before trying to take anything off his person. And with two murders on their hands, it wouldn't surprise me if the police had us all stripping to our scivvies before the night was over. Yeah, that intriguing little message would be much safer with Kareem.

As we started to leave, I turned to Lydia and said, "Look, I think I believe what little you've told me so far. So whatever, do not tell the police anything. Not yet. Don't deny anything. Don't admit anything. Don't volunteer a blessed thing, okay?"

She fully understood, and the three of us left the cottage to see what other exciting things were happening to the aged Hornet Hummers.

7

I took an immediate and gross dislike towards Lieutenant Percy A. Burnside, not only because he was an arrogant bastard, but because he is one of those under-achiever types who takes out his frustration and anxiety on those who have made it to the rung he couldn't quite reach. This sort of personality, given every equal chance to run a foot race with someone as ideally and fairly matched as possible, would piss and moan relentlessly if he found himself coming in second at the tape. "Oh yeah, well, you had *Adidas* sneakers ... mine were just these worn-out old things from Monkey Wards." Or, "Well, of course *you* won — you had a bigger cheering section."

I just cannot tolerate a snivelling s.o.b. like that, or the snide innuendos they love to interject at every chance, so it was not long after Lieutenant Burnside made clear his offensive demeanor that I said, "Look, Lieutenant, I appreciate the fact that we've had a terrible thing happen here, and that it's your job to find out exactly who's responsible, but we also have a whole lot of nice people here — all of whom have travelled quite some distance. Right now they're frightened, uncomfortable, and I will not tolerate your bullying them, making nasty little remarks or otherwise making anyone needlessly agitated. Do you understand?"

This outburst had been prompted by my overhearing Burnside brow-beating little Carlita after it was learned she was the last to see Arbaugh alive.

Burnside considered me for a moment, not sure if he should press his luck. Then a veil descended over his face, and I knew I'd not have any more trouble with him. I was mentally dusting my hands off, when I realized that Kareem was standing beside me, and had no doubt glared at Burnside, punctuating my little diatribe.

Ernie Tucker was our second hapless victim. Someone had knocked him unconscious, stuffed him in the front of one of my favorite cars, the forty-seven Cadillac convertible which was tucked at the far end of the garage. Then, with the engine running, and the doors closed, Ernie went to that big bank vault in the sky. At least he went in style.

I suppose I could be considered an accessory before the fact, in that I'd left everything unlocked and had told the guests where the car keys board was if they wanted to take any of the twelve old beasts for a spin. Evidently, someone did want to hear the Caddy purr a little. It was the sound of the engine, as its exhaust asphyxiated Ernie, that had attracted a few of Lydia's searchers into the garage, including Chad Carter and Robert, Artie Younger and Clarence Hildahl. It was poor Artie who dragged Ernie's body out and tried unsuccessfully to resuscitate him. He didn't have anything funny to say about that.

Official police photographers busied themselves recording for all time the corpses, the surrounding premises, and a couple of times, I think they accidentally took a snap or two of each other in action.

Individual statements were taken from all the guests, and by midnight Lieutenant Burnside ceremoniously and with great relish mounted the platform and spoke into the microphone, evidently his first such experience, as it looked like he might swallow it. "One — two — three — testing. Uh ... ladies and gentlemen, I'm police Lieutenant Percy A. Burnside, homicide ... could I have your attention ... yes, uh, we got us a double murder here, uh, the deceased being ..." He referred to a piece of paper, "One Paul Joseph Arbaugh, age thirty-eight ... and one Ernest William Tucker, age thirty-nine. Cause of death has yet to be officially determined.

"I don't mean to alarm you, but it does look like there's a killer on the loose here, ladies and gentlemen, so not only must I caution each of you to be extra careful ..." The crowd started talking and worrying aloud. "... uh, could I have your attention ... *please!* Thank you. Uh, I'll have to ask all of you to remain here tonight while we continue our investigation.

"Now, I know that you're all from out of town, and I've gotten permission to stay here with my men as long as it takes to get to the bottom of this thing, so's not to inconvenience anyone unduly."

Someone shouted, "What if you don't find the killer by tomorrow, Lieutenant? Most of us got to get back home and to our jobs — we don't all live fancy-rich like Derek, here." The crowd gave off a nervous laugh. How quickly they turn, I mused.

"Well, we're going to do everything the best way we can, folks, but if we don't nab the killer by tomorrow ..." But he sensed the rising resentment in the crowd, "... maybe we'll take depositions or something. I don't know — I'll have to check with my department head on that."

Right then, Kareem hailed the Lieutenant away from the microphone and then had a little confab off to one side. Presently, the Lieutenant returned to the microphone. "Uh ... ladies and gentlemen, I have some good news and some bad news, as the saying goes." No one seemed amused. "Uh, because we know approximately when the first victim was killed, uh ... one Paul Joseph Arbaugh, age thirty-eight ... he was among the first to receive some sort

of award or something, I guess ... you know more
about that right now than I do ... his name was
second on the alphabetical list, and the others were
given after him ... and then Mr. Dax was to be up
next ...

"But that's when news of the first deceased body
was announced ... right? Well, Mr. Khan here, tells
me there were a number of you out there taking
pictures of the people getting these awards, and he
suggests that if you'd bring us all your cameras we
could have the film developed and see just who was
standing up here where I am now, or in the
immediate area — and that way we'll be pretty sure
who can be allowed to leave. That might eliminate
some of the suspects right off, since you couldn't be
here getting an award or something, and out in the
pool area murdering somebody at the same time. So,
if you'd bring your cameras up here and place them
on the table ..."

Inside of twenty minutes there was a big pile of
cameras, plus a stack of Polaroids and instant
Kodak snaps on the table.

At my suggestion, the Lieutenant and a couple
of his staff, plus Kareem and myself moved
everything to the library, and then Kareem with one
of the Lieutenant's boys went off to his private
darkroom to develop the pictures from the roll film
cameras.

Burnside, the other fellow and I, spread the

instant photographs out on my desk and I started to make a list, identifying each of the people in the pictures by name. The five piece combo had struck up a tension-easing rendition of "Yellow Submarine," and I could hear a few strains of the tune as the door to the library burst open, and Lydia, followed closely by a man, came running towards me. She fell into my arms and cried, "Oh Derek, make them stop! I cannot take any more."

The man behind her said dumbly, "I was just doing my job — I've got to ask her questions, hell, she's our chief suspect!"

I looked at him directly, still holding Lydia and ordered, "Out! Get the hell out! *Now!* And to Burnside, I said, "I told you, Burnside — I don't want any rough stuff or harrassment. These people are my guests, and I do not associate with riff-raff ... normally." I let the implication sink in as deeply as possible.

Quietly but firmly he directed the fellow to leave, just as Kareem walked in with the prints, still very damp and separated by waxed sheets.

We completed our chore of scanning the photos, and identifying the people, and Burnside made a point of noting, as if surprised, that I was in several of the scenes, and then made an even greater issue of the fact Lydia Arbaugh was in none. Upon hearing this, she started to explain why she was not present when her husband's or any of the other's prophecies were read, but I caught her attention and she remained silent.

"Okay, ladies and gentlemen. This is Lieutenant Burnside, again. I got that good news and bad news I mentioned earlier." Still no signs of amusement. He needs a new jokewriter. "Uh, following here is a list of people who I got to ask to stay for an indefinite period, 'cause you're not in any of the pictures we've looked at. I'll read your names off and the rest of you can go, in fact, it would be a good idea if you did, 'cause you might just be in the way otherwise.

"Uh, when you leave though, my men here will take your names, and where you're staying tonight, and also they'll need your home address, and some proof of it. Driver's license, i.d., or whatever you got. We may need to get ahold of you at your hotels or at your homes after you get back to 'em. Just routine."

As names of the captives were read off, it was an utterly fascinating study of human nature to see the group gradually divide into two factions, each with members of common bond within their newly split sphere, and each with its unspoken and sudden animosity for the other. Hours before, these were a people laughing and loving each other, but now, the lines were being drawn. "They" are suspected murders — we are not. "They" think we're murderers, but how do we know they're not — since we know we aren't ...

There were nervous and not too polite parting

words between the larger group allowed to leave, and the smaller one required to remain, although Artie Younger, who had been in most every picture and was thus free to go, broke the tension by shouting, "Hey, you guys — I know you didn't ice anybody — but whoever is guilty, I wish you'd give me a call when you're in my neighborhood — maybe you could drum up some fresh business for me!"

Phyllis, although not a suspect, remained with the others which I'm sure she would have done even if she hadn't been staying at the house as my personal guest. She was very supportive of everyone, flitting about, raising spirits — it was almost like everyone was facing some impending doom, and she felt compelled to lift their spirits to help them see it through. In a sense, that was the case.

We made arrangements for the group — some twenty nine in all, to stay the night, with only a small amount of doubling up in the bedrooms being necessary. One by one, throughout the night, Lieutenant Burnside and his cohorts paraded the suspects into the library, put them through extensive interrogation, and then out they'd come, looking pale and worried.

"This is all simply ghastly! I don't see why little Paulie had to go and get himself killed, and ruin our grand party, do you? And poor old Ernie, too. Those men in there are just beasts — but I guess they're just doing their job. The short one's kind of cute though, don't you think, Derek? Well, I suppose *you* wouldn't notice, though."

"Chad, you should have cured your pimples back in high school the way the rest of us did!"

"Oh, how ever did you do that ... yes, I did have quite a crop of zits as a child."

"By screwing girls, Chad — by screwing *girls!*"

For a moment I thought he was going to melt into the floor like the witch in the "Wizard of Oz."

Lydia came by and said, Goodnight, the police had decided to wait until morning to question her further, and I said, for Chad's benefit, "Goodnight, Mrs. Arbaugh. If you have trouble sleeping, you may want to go for a stroll on the grounds and smell the lotus." Her eyes told me she understood, and she said goodnight to both Chad and myself.

"A real foxy bitch, that." Chad snorted as Lydia walked down the hall.

"So are you, Chad — minus the foxy part." And I hastened off to the cottage.

"We'd better leave the lights out, Lydia — just in case someone is prowling around. I hoped you'd connect my remark about sniffing the lotus with the cottage. Since you'd read the book, I thought you might."

"Is the car, Penelope's Lotus, still here?"

"It's up at the house, in the garage, that is, with my cars. I offered to buy it, but Penelope said no, just use it and keep it happy until she got out."

"When will that be, Derek?"

I sensed that she was somehow putting herself in the shoes of another woman convicted of murdering her husband, so I replied, "Hey Lydia, forget all that. Let's not have you concerned about doing time in prison when you're not even guilty."

"Are you sure of that"

"Relatively, yes. The note from Paul was addressed to me, and in his handwriting as best we can determine. It clearly stated that he thought he would meet an untimely death, and in that event, he was asking me to look after your welfare. Words to that effect. I got only the gist of it before handing the note to Kareem for safe keeping. But above all, I remember verbatim, Paul's closing remark; 'Listen to Lydia. Believe her. Trust her. She knows.' *What* do you know, Lydia?"

"All right. I must tell you, but also I warn you; it will sound incredible at first, yet, if you accept what I say as the truth, ultimately it will be so deceptively simple that, perhaps like Paul often did, you'll feel like pounding your fists or beating your head on the wall.

"Some years back, I went to work for Paul as a research assistant. He was a full professor at Tech then, and I was a graduate student. We worked together and fell in love. Paul was a marvelous human being — much more full of life and good humor then.

"What was your field? Yours and his, I mean."

"Micro-biology — but oddly enough, that had nothing to do with any of this, although Paul's analytical mind and infinite curiosity led to ... now. His death."

"Go on."

"After we adoted Daniel, I quit working with Paul on a regular basis. Daniel wasn't a baby or anything, he was nearly four, but he'd come from a terribly abusive background, and he needed all the constant love and attention that I could give him as a mother. It may have been the child's influence — to perpetuate and protect one's offspring, I don't know, but one night as we were watching the news, the only television Paul would ever watch, his face became animated and he stood up and shouted, 'Damn the blasted oil companies! Damn the government! It's all a crock! People are killing each other just trying to get gas for their cars! Businesses are going broke! Old people are going to freeze next winter and boil to death in the summer!'

"He went over to little Daniel, picked him up lovingly and said aloud, 'And what's to become of you? If the energy shortage is real — it'll be gone by the time you need it — and if it's all contrived ... well, I'll fix the bastards!' And he stalked off to his little shop out in back. I had never ever seen him in such a fit of uncontrollable rage. It scared me, and scared the boy."

"What happened?"

"Well, I just sort of sat there the rest of the evening. About midnight, he came into the house, looking very tired and withdrawn. I knew that he'd been running his brain on overtime as he referred to his think sessions. Often, in the earlier years, we'd have such sessions together. Oh, I'm not a genius like Paul was or anything, but it helped him to have me around when he had a particularly difficult problem or equasion confronting him. I acted as his sounding-board, I guess.

"That night, when he came in, he came over to the couch where I sat, dropped a rumpled sheet on the cocktail table and sat next to me, exhausted. I asked him, 'What is it, Paul?' and he just laughed, a sickening sort of laugh, if you know what I mean. He was obviously very dejected. He said, 'Lydia, before you lies the answer to this nation's — no, this *world's* basic energy crisis — but the funny thing is, we can't do a damn thing about it — in fact, I'll have to destroy that.' He reached for a table lighter and started to ignite the sheet.

"I implored him to wait and to first tell me what he was talking about. He started, by saying that I probably wouldn't believe it at first, yet he had proved out his theory with extensive mathematical computations, and he knew he was correct ... he had found a solution to the principal thief of our world energy supply — the automobile."

"And he had that all figured out on a single piece of paper?" My disbelief was quite evident.

"Yes, he did. He said that like most highly complex problems, the solution was really quite simple. It was lying there before anyone's eyes — not just highly skilled scientists and engineers — but anyone. And when he showed me his little draft, I too, could see the pure logic of this thesis."

"Which was?"

"Well, I can show you, if you like, and perhaps I should, so you'll believe the rest of what I have to say." Lydia cast about for a pen and paper, the latter being a yellow paper napkin, slightly coffee stained. I turned on a small table lamp.

"Okay. Now there are the four wheels of the car. They are attached to a more or less regular sort of automobile frame — with a few minor, but insignificant alterations for our purposes here. Basically, as Paul explained it, a front wheel drive car such as a Honda or a Subaru would be the simplest and best to work with on a prototype.

"In the front, the gasoline engine would be replaced by a large electric motor, controlled by a rheostat. The drive portion of the motor would be connected to a regular transmission configuration — automatic or manual shift, so that the feel of driving would be much the same as a conventionally powered car. Paul felt that important for the concept to gain acceptance with the driving public."

"You're saying he wanted to build an electric car. So what."

"Oh no. It's not an electric car in the usual sense. Look: Built into the side frames or anywhere else for that matter, are a series of heavy-duty storage batteries. Notice I said *storage* batteries. Now, in the rear of the car is another motor, similar in size to the one in the front, but it is wound in reverse, making it a giant ..."

"Generator."

"Correct. The generator is linked by a simple clutch and gear arrangement to the back left wheel here," Lydia drew a few lines as the spoke, "and the generator is wired to the batteries, the batteries to the motor, and ... voila! A self-perpetuating, non-polluting, no-energy consumptive vehicle. There's a capacitor and a voltmeter and some other do-dads that go in here somewhere, but basically that's the set-up.

"Paul was able to circumvent the law of physics governing the friction and resistance impediment to the generator by designing some freewheeling bearing modules for the wheels, plus a series of cut-off devices which allowed the generator to run free of the linkage as much as possible. It would engage and thus subject itself to drag only when the sensing device indicated additional input was required in the storage batteries."

"Essentially then, if it worked, a person would never have to buy another gallon of gas, or oil, or anti-freeze, or ... need a radiator, or ..."

"Or a muffler and tail pipes ... or the brackets to fasten any of that stuff onto the car or anything else in the multi-billion dollar primary, secondary or aftermarket supported by the standard internal combustion engine."

"So, I see. Paul reasoned, quite logically, I fear, that if his simple but ingenius development became known, any number of rich and powerful people, firms or even entire nations would be down his neck wanting to kill the idea or even him, rather than see the concept come into fruition and become the catalyst for a total rebirth of the automobile industry."

"Exactly."

"So, he burned the sketch, and decided against making his discovery known. I hate to say it, but considering the many potential repercussions, he made a wise decision."

"He burned the sketch." Lydia's voice was hollow, yet told me there was more.

"He burned the sketch, but ...?"

"He built the car."

"He built *that* car?"

"It was my fault, really. I could see the tremendous benefits to all of mankind. No more anguish over the ever-worsening oil crisis, the political unrest, people literally going hungry to keep themselves warm or to buy gas for their cars — no more reports of people commiting suicide when their little businesses failed because of all sorts of problems created by the whole energy mess ...

"... so, I convinced him it was his civic duty — those were my stupid, childish words, 'civic duty' to make the concept work — prove it — and give it to mankind. He didn't want money for it. The thought never entered his mind. He didn't even want personal recognition. He just wanted it *to be*. And so did I."

"What did he do?"

"Well, he had a friend at an Oregon University who was more familiar with the current state-of-the-art in the field of electric powered transportation, so he contacted him. He came out to St. Louis — that's where we live, I didn't know if you knew that — and in about two months they actually had their prototype. It was a regular-looking nineteen seventy three Subaru wagon, an ugly mustard-colored thing ... and it worked. Exactly as Paul had said it would.

"We would drive that thing all over at any speed up to eighty miles an hour, and no matter what, the batteries never lost their charge. They would just automatically be recharged by the car's own generator, and as I say, the generator was in turn driven by the back wheel and the connecting

gearage. The average person, the layman, would no
doubt look upon this as some sort of impossible
perpetual motion machine, but of course it was not
that at all, but rather, a scientific instrument
transformed into a practical, working apparatus."

"So what did they do with the car?"

"Justin — that was my husband's friend — had
been after Paul to let him try to work a deal with one
of the big electronics firms — to sell the idea to them
for development commercially. That seemed logical, except as Paul pointed out, the thing was *too* big
— no one could really be trusted when it came to the
potential billions of dollars at stake — both to be
gained and lost. Not a lawyer, not a politician, not
anybody.

"Even a firm standing to gain financially by
developing the concept might be swayed by even
bigger monies from special interest groups who
stood to *lose* huge sums when the thing went into
production. The oil companies, the manufacturers
of all the accessories no longer required on such a
vehicle, and others. He felt then, that the only thing
to do was either to scrap the whole project and forget
it — and he could do that, now that he'd proved to
himself the viability of the concept — or, to send it
directly to the Department of Energy here in
Washington with as much public and press fanfare
as possible. He felt that was far safer than being
secretive about it, or trying to make behind-closed-

doors deals with manufacturers.

"But even the idea of bringing the invention to the attention of the Washington bureaucrats didn't appeal to Paul, as he was convinced that given today's technology, the unlimited financial resources of our government, and the supposed world energy crisis, some solution, similar or even superior to his own, could already have been created, but had been quashed by the powers-that-be. He was a bit paranoid perhaps, but then maybe he just saw things as they really are ...

"In any event, Paul and Justin maintained their on-going argument for several days after the car was built and functioning."

"What happened then?"

"He killed him. Paul killed Justin. Oh, it was sort of accidental, but I know Paul was relieved. Justin had been away from his wife for nearly three months, and one day when Paul was away, he made some serious advances towards me. I didn't really blame him in one sense, I could understand his natural urges given the length of time he'd been away from home, but of course, I refused him. But he was determined, and ... forced me to have intercourse with him.

"When I realized there was nothing else I could do, I submitted, and frankly, tried to make the experience bearable for him as well as myself, since I knew his conscience would be enough for him to live with afterwards."

"And ...?"

"Paul came in on us ... dragged Justin away, but Justin hit his head on a nearby table and died instantly."

"Was there a trial or what?"

"No, Paul took the body out to the country that night and buried it. It was never found."

I sighed heavily. This plot was getting a tad murky. "The car?"

"I don't know. Paul wouldn't tell me. He said I was better off not knowing. Two days after Justin's death, the calls began. An anonymous man said enough to Paul to indicate that he knew a lot about his invention, that he'd been dealing with Paul's partner, as he called him and wanted to make a deal. Paul pretended ignorance, but the man continued to harass us for several weeks.

"Then, all of a sudden he stopped. Paul became very agitated during that period, but then seemed to resolve himself to the inevitable. He became withdrawn and maudlin. He increased his life insurance policy, started attending to all sorts of loose ends, as he called them, all in preparation for his own death. Somehow, he seemed confident that I would be safe, as well as Daniel, as he reasoned that Justin would never have revealed the simplicity of the concept when bargaining, so whoever knew of its existence would not suspect that I, a mere housewife, would have any knowledge or under-standing of the design."

"I assume then that you think the person who called your husband killed him? Why would he do that?"

"Well, Paul couldn't be bought off — either to sell his idea, or to destroy it. So his idea had to be destroyed. That meant killing him, because he had probably been unsuccessful in making it clear to the caller that the car didn't exist anymore, or that the concept was invalid, that he and his associate, Justin, had scratched further research. I heard him tell the man those things a couple of times and also that Justin had returned to the coast. Then, as I say, the calls stopped."

"And that was that."

"Except for the continuing fear that Paul had for his life — not unjustified, obviously."

"May I ask why you're not more visibly shaken by your husband's death, Lydia? You haven't cried once that I know of since learning about it."

"I don't know the answer to that exactly. I loved Paul. I truly loved him. But he's dead, almost precisely as a proven equasion that he might have chalked on the board. I will weep, I suppose — in time. But not now."

I didn't press the issue — what business is it of mine? The hour was late, and I walked Lydia Arbaugh back to the main house and went in search of Kareem.

8

I had left Lydia at the entrance to the garden so as not to appear conspicuous as her escort. Burnside was mostly convinced, I thought, that I was not a serious murder suspect, but if he saw me with Lydia he might 'jump to collusion' with his prime suspect, and thus curtail my access to whatever little inside data was being assembled on the case.

I overheard low voices coming from a secluded area of the garden, and peered through a small quince to ascertain who might still be out at this late hour. In the shadows, I saw a man and woman sitting on one of the benches situated in the outer perimeter of the garden. When I saw that the man had his hand under the woman's dress, actively stimulating both her and himself, I smiled and moved away. I'll sit through a stag movie now and then like any other red-blooded man ... or woman, for that matter, but generally, I do not invade other's privacy in real life. But ...

... something was not registering correctly in

my tired brain, so I looked back again at the couple. By now, he had her on the grassy surface next to the bench, her dress pulled high above her waist. As he started to enter her, I stood transfixed in utter fascination at the sight. It was unmistakeably Aloice Peterson, the Hornet Hummers hopeful for first woman in space, being quite admirably dorked by none other than Chad Carter, our class queer, who now appeared to be thoroughly and expertly enjoying what to him, I suppose could only be termed forbidden fruit.

★ ★ ★ ★

"Kareem, there you are, could we go someplace private and talk?"

"Let's go to my room. You haven't seen it since I moved in, anyway."

Kareem had, for his own reasons, selected just two rooms on the third floor of the mansion, each quite small compared to the many rooms he could as easily have had if he wanted them. The first was a sitting room of sorts, furnished with plain but comfortable fabric-covered furniture. The room beyond was his bedroom with a full bath adjacent.

When in residence, he took his meals down-stairs, often with myself if I were in town, although we had no structured arrangement in that regard as neither of us cares to be restricted to exact schedules for dining or anything else.

As we entered the room, I was pleased to see that a painter's easel dominated one corner, prevailing over which was a huge skylight. The only one in the entire house.

"Now I know why you insisted on this tiny grouping of rooms, Kareem — you *have* started painting again! Great! Can I see what you're working on ..." I started to walk towards the painting-in-progress.

"No! Please, not yet ..."

"Okay, sure. I don't like anyone reading my scripts whilst they're in progress, either. I understand. Listen, let's sit down then, and discuss this matter."

"Our case."

"You insist on making us out as super sleuths, don't you my friend."

"Well, we are. There was the Brisbane case that started you on your new sideline career, and then those three or four times that you aided me in my domestic assignments, and now this caper."

I smiled at the way he said caper. "You watch too much teevee, Kareem" indicating the darkened Sony perched ludicrously on the marble mantelpiece. "By the way, after that last 'caper' — the Finkbine kidnapping fiasco — I resolved to have you teach me a little of your 'Pakistani Parachutist Karate' moves, but we've never gotten around to it. I didn't appreciate getting my socks knocked off by that big bozo, you know? If I knew a few of your moves I could have averted that."

"I will teach you my tricks as soon as we can get the time, Mr. Dax."

"Well, some of them, at least. I'm really not sure about wanting to become a killing machine like you — just a few defensive tactics, okay?"

Kareem's face was expressionless, and I knew that I'd offended him, but he quickly shot me a forgiving look.

"Okay, on this caper, then ..." and I related the full incredible story Lydia had told me, and also the strange scene I'd peeping-tommed in the garden, and ended with another strange observation just now retrieved from my mental file.

"Say, I remember now what it was that didn't jive in with the total picture of everybody milling about after Arbaugh's body was pulled from the pool. Where are those pix you took with the Nikon?"

"Okay, look — there's Doc Wilson in the pool with Arbaugh's body, and there also are Victor Louden, the little guy, and the bald one, that's Clarence Hildah. By the way, he's just returned from Saudi Arabia — that sounds overly suspicious, wouldn't you say — given the electric car deal, and all?"

"Perhaps, but 'what's wrong with this picture' as your American magazine puzzles used to say?"

"You remember those, do you? Those were kind of fun ... uh, the thing is, there we have Wilson, Louden and Hildahl in the pool with Arbaugh, but ..."

"But what?"

"No Artie Younger."

"The funny undertaker?"

"Yeah. He's not there in the picture, but sometime during the fracas I noticed that his lower trouser legs were wet or at least damp. How'd they get that way, if he didn't jump in the pool with the others ...? Yet, he couldn't have done in Arbaugh 'cause he's in every single picture that was taken during the prophecy reading ..."

"Look at this — you may find it rather interesting, as well." Kareem produced the packet.

"Oh yes, the prophecies. I noticed you grabbed those off the table. I'm surprised Burnside hasn't appropriated these."

"He didn't ask for them."

I paged through the stack, pausing to read my own rather carefully. "I'll be damned. When I told Phyllis that I'd thought I would someday be a movie star, I really didn't remember that twenty years ago I was actually serious and wrote it all down right here ..."

"I know, I read it. But look at the others."

I shuffled through, glancing at the projected aspirations of my fellow classmates. Many contained fervent and idyllic hopes along the lines of "A world united in peace with lasting brotherhood for everyone." Sounds like a contestant at a Miss America pageant giving her all. There was Edgar Johnson, stating unequivocally that he would, at the time of this reading, be a world-revered surgeon. He was certain. There was not a trace of doubt in his wording. What did Edger tell me he does ... an electrician, I think. Probably much happier and richer doing that, anyway.

I passed through the others, not bothering to read more than a line or two. In a way, since we were not all sharing the experience, I felt a bit ill at ease, like I was reading someone else's mail. Then, not knowing at the moment exactly why, I separated one of the sheets from the rest, and studied it carefully. There were the customary snappy phrases at the start, a few lines extolling the good times at Coolidge High, and then, "As I can see no finer way to benefit mankind, or any better method to fully put to use my extraordinary and varied talents, I will strive to become one half of the world's first outerspace copulating couple, and to that end predict that as this prophecy is being read at our twenty year class reunion in Coolidge High gymnasium, all of you hearing these words will in fact know that Aloice Peterson and I have endeared ourselves as history's first intergalactic, intercoursing twosome, orbiting the earth's atmosphere in our little Gemini spacecraft, blissfully and historically."

"The paper ... it's not as yellowed as the others. There's an acid used in the manufacturing process that causes paper to discolor with age, if I recall anything of my father's tutelage of the printing craft ..."

"You would notice *that*. I didn't, to tell you the truth, but I did pick up on something else most interesting on that particular prophecy. Do you see it ...?"

I looked again at the words, instead of the paper, and re-read the whole text, closing with, 'orbiting the earth's atmosphere in our little Gemini spacecraft, blissfully and historically.' *"Gemini spacecraft.* But, of course! Do you have an encyclopedia in here, Kareem?"

"Don't need one. The Gemini was the second stage of the American space program — long after this was supposedly written. If it had said Mercury spacecraft, then it would have figured, but not Gemini — that was long after the prophecies were written and sealed away. This particular one had to be written only after — maybe long after the others, according to your yellowing disclosure — no doubt to replace the original one which probably in some way was incriminating."

"Or embarrassing. Maybe the guy just wanted to avoid some hassle with his wife, or a friend. I mean, maybe in the original prophecy he said something which later seemed a bit overt, like spending the next twenty years screwing so and so. That could be, given the racy language used in the replacement copy here. Maybe so and so — the object of his intentions — was somebody who later married a good friend or something. Or perhaps she was one of the girls who has died in the interim, and he thought such a risque statement might now be vulgar. Hell, maybe he was actually having a thing with one of the girls back in school, wrote his little piece describing it or something, and then later decided that discretion was the better part of valor, and persuaded Ernie Tucker to let him make a switch in the prophecy parcel."

"Tucker is dead."

"Yeah, that's pretty strong persuasion, eh wot? But that wouldn't tie in with Arbaugh's murder. No, I think this thing here, the switched prophecy, is a trifle — something to overlook if we are going to get to the bottom of the actual murders."

"Could be, but I've asked some of my friends to do a little checking here and there. Discreetly, of course."

"Oh, but of course, how else ..."

We decided to call it quits for the night — actually it was four A.M., and I bade Kareem goodnight and headed for my room. Phyllis was in my bed, sound asleep. I undressed and slipped under the covers next to her, but she merely rolled over, snored once or twice and continued her slumber uninterrupted by any serious unfaithfulness to good old Fred, babysitting the grandkiddies back home.

In the morning, she was gone, but this time I was quite sure I'd not dreamed the incident. There was a scribbled note on the pillow next to me which had just one word, 'Great!', with the signature, 'P.'

During breakfast, we all appeared as one humungous happy family, with Carlita, Serenity and the hired servants piling huge portions of scrambled eggs, bacon and hotcakes on everybody's plate. The Lieutenant and his men joined the rest of us, and had anyone dropped in in the middle of this morning feast and overheard all the nice conversation, they would never have suspected that a double murder investigation was going on.

"After breakfast, I'd appreciate your taking a few minutes away from your guests, Mr. Dax. I'd like a few words in private. Also, the big gentleman, if he's available."

"Kareem? Yes, I'm certain he's up and about somewhere. He doesn't eat breakfast, which is probably whe he's not here."

But we couldn't seem to find Kareem, and Serenity volunteered to me privately that he had left several hours before, but told her he would be back around breakfast time. Burnside told those gathered at breakfast that they were free to enjoy the day, and in response to several who asked, said that the investigation was nearly over, that he thought he knew who the killer was, and that before the day was ended the killer's career would be, too. That's exactly what he said, so help me.

"Listen, Mr. Dax ... I haven't the damndest notion of who the killer is, and this thing is getting crazier all the time! I'm telling you this in confidence, because I've done a little checking on you and your big friend, and I believe you can be trusted. Where is he, by the way?"

"Kareem? Oh, he's off doing a little sleuthing on his own, I imagine."

"Well, just so's he gets back here pretty soon. Anyway, I want you to look at these autopsy reports and you'll see what I mean about this thing getting crazier, but ..." He handed me the files, "my showing you these is unofficial, off the record so to speak, okay?"

I agreed and started scanning the reports, skipping all the preliminary stuff covering the physical description of the corpses and other incidental observations of the pathologist.

"Kareem was right. Arbaugh died from the knife wound to the heart — dead center, according to this — not from drowning. So, as we figured, whoever killed Paul with a knife, actually a nasty looking stiletto, dumped the body in the pool. Why though, I don't see."

"We're thinking that maybe the deceased was

attacked somewhere in the vicinity of the pool, left for dead, and then tried to crawl to the house but fell into the pool accidentally. There was some excess moisture in the lungs as you can see from the report even though it was the toad stabber that was fatal."

"Did you find any traces of blood in the area surrounding the pool?"

"No ... but the nature of the puncture wound precluded any copious blood flow, and as you know, your pals were churning up the water around there pretty good when they dragged the body out, so they could've washed away any drops of blood if there were any."

"That makes sense, I suppose. The stiletto, anything about that which leads anywhere?"

"Naw. No prints. Nothing especially unusual about the thing. There are a million or more like it — they're imported from Taiwan by the shipload. Wouldn't even pay to try tracing it.

"I'll level with you about what really bugs me with Arbaugh ... I can't find any real reason for someone doin' him in. He wasn't rich. He and his wife seemed to have a normal relationship from best we can determine, both from talking with her and from the little data we've been able to obtain from the Saint Louie department ... She's quite a lady, that Mrs. Arbaugh ..." Burnside failed to conceal his interest in what my reaction to that fishing exhibition might be.

"Indeed, she is quite a lady, Lieutenant. Vivacious, charming, sexually alluring and several years junior to Arbaugh. She might even be worth killing for if a person were so inclined — but I was not. Does that peg it for you, Lieutenant?" I smiled at my little victory.

"Yeah, well, then there's the other victim, Tucker. Now, he was a banker ... money, possibly a disgruntled customer, someone whose loan he called in, maybe ..."

"Ernie was a small town banker, son of a small town banker, and believe me, I grew up there and everybody knows everybody else's business there, Lieutenant. I really doubt if any skullduggery could go on without everybody knowing about it — and the few folks who still live there and knew Ernie — from our high school class, I mean — are here, and unless you got some scoop or something ..."

"Naw, not really. They told me about Tucker's father gettin' killed in an explosion at the bank several years back, but I guess that was just a leaking gas main or something."

"But look at this ..." I was reading the reports again. "Isn't that interesting. Tucker didn't really die from the carbon monoxide or even the rap on the head, according to this. The coroner thinks he was strangled. Geez, somebody wanted to make damn sure he was a goner. They konked him on the bean, strangled him and then for good measure stuffed him in my Caddy and fumigated him for awhile ..."

"Yeah, yeah. But what's got me stuck is who and why? Unless we got a psycho runnin' around your house killing off people just for the fun of it, none of the pieces fit. Only a couple or so of your old classmates have even kept in touch with each other. Christmas cards, and a couple folks remembering birthdays — that sort of thing. These people are scattered all over, as well. I can't find any common link between 'em at all, other than twenty years ago you all graduated from the same school. But then the connection gets very weak. Like I said, Mr. Dax, I'm tellin' you all this on the sly, 'cause I'm stumped right now, and thought maybe you could shed some light on the proceedings."

I debated with myself about telling him what I knew concerning Arbaugh's invention, and the rest of that mess, but decided against it. If it did not become really vital to solving these crimes, why divulge that Lydia Arbaugh, herself a quasi-willing rape victim, was now the widow of a murder victim, himself a murderer. Was it really necessary to heap all that on her as well as on her young son? Maybe it would be later, but not yet. "No, I can't really see any motive for the killings, Lieutenant."

He didn't look like I'd convinced him of that, or he was simply disappointed because I was unable to offer him any help after he'd as much as admitted he didn't know where the hell to go from here, and so he bristled, "Okay, so you haven't got any ideas, but I'll tell you this, Mr. Dax, one or more of your guests out there sitting right in your house is a murderer, plain and simple. I don't know if it's a man or a woman, if he kills for fun, money, revenge or what, but that killer is out there — maybe just waiting for a chance to kill someone else. Maybe even *you!*"

I wished he hadn't said that, because it would be difficult to write a story about all this if I were dead, and this thing was starting to shape up as a most interesting plot line, indeed.

9

"So, why'd you leave the place, Kareem? It's Sunday, most everything's closed, and if you wanted to call someone, at last count I think we've got three dozen phones or more scattered around the joint ..."

"They're bugged."

"The phones? *My* phones are bugged?"

"Yes. I checked them last night."

"Who? The police?"

"Probably. Oh, don't get all riled up — you can't blame them. They've got a lot of suspects here — and four times that many people have already left the premises. Who knows who might be calling whom, and what information might be exchanged. It was a good move. I would have done it too, if I was Burnside."

"Okay, so you went out to an unbugged phone. And ..."

"Not much, yet. I just made some contacts with a few more friends. Asked them to check out a few things."

"You were gone a long time." I sounded like a cuckholded husband."

"But, of course. We have a lot of suspects."

"You know, Kareem, this whole thing is going to be a whole lot easier to comprehend, and especially to write about with the benefit of hindsight, than it is right now."

"Don't tell me, that after all the books you've written you're having trouble figuring out where to go from here, again ... didn't that same thing happen to you in *"The Enchanted Cottage"* when we were on our way up to the mansion from the cottage just before discovering ..."

"Hush! Don't say it — maybe the guy reading *this* one hasn't yet experienced *"The Enchanted Cottage"* — so why spoil it for them? Yeah, I did have a moment or two there where I realized that we have such a fantastically clever and involved plot development going on, that it was hard to decide just which way to take it from here — but I'm sure I, we, can work it out quite spectacularly. You game?"

"Hey — *you're* pushing the pen, boss — you tell *me!*"

"Okay, we're going to do it then — just hang in there a tad longer, okay?"

"You can do whatever you want — just don't have anybody thump me on my tender jaw again — that really was embarrassing the last time — the way you had me sprawled out unconscious like that."

"I make no promises — this is a risky business, eh wot?"

"Yeah, and one of those risks is an uninspired editor who just can't see how something like this, right now, could possibly work and so he reaches for the blue pencil ..."

"If he does, I'll sic the Pakistani brown hulk on his case ..."

Kareem's delighted little tee-hee, tee-hee snapped me from my spate of daydreaming, and we were able to return to a more or less sane posture.

10

The balance of the morning and earlier portion of the afternoon were taken up by further interrogations of each of the remaining guests, and Burnside, just to exert his authority, I suspect (and also because I could use the benefit of the extra words on this page) had his men round up a half dozen or so of the guests he'd allowed to leave the previous night.

Around three, we were gathered outside on the patio, enjoying a mid afternoon snack and cocktails. A couple of the girls had gotten together to put on a senseless but amusing little musical, and were dancing and singing their joyous little hearts out.

I singled out Aloice Peterson and asked her if she'd care to go for a stroll and she readily agreed. I directed her out through the garden and past the horse stables, and asked if she'd care to ride but she declined. I am so glad, because I have personally never been on one of the beasts in my life, and had she accepted I'd now have to spend a couple hours of research to make the event sound realistic. So we walked. I asked her if she'd been down to the cottage.

"No, but I'd be glad to see it. That's where you do all your writing, and some of your loving, isn't it, Derek?" Her manner was teasing, but I sensed a not well-hidden invitation as well.

"Oh yeah, a little of each, I guess, but from what I saw last night you're pretty well squared away in the loving department yourself." She stopped walking, and I looked to see what her reaction might be. "I didn't mean to peek — I was coming back late, and heard a noise, and saw you and Chad going at it fairly enthusiastically."

"You wouldn't tell, would you, Derek?" She sounded scared and childlike.

"Hey, Aloice — you're a grown-up — what you do is your business. No, I'm not going to squeal on you. Who would I tell, anyway?"

"The others ... oh, anybody — I don't know. I don't want any of the other kids to know about that or anything else. I ..." And she began to sob a little. We were some distance from the cottage, so I urged her over to a small grove of poplars, and we sat down in the shade.

"You want to tell me?"

"Yeah, I think I would." She paused. "Back in school, I really did want to be the first lady astronaut. I know everybody thought it was a joke, but it wasn't. I was dead serious. So, after graduation, like most everbody else, I up and left to seek my fortune." She laughed derisively, "My fortune. Ha!"

"Where'd you go?"

"Cape Canaveral, where else? They called it Cape Kennedy later, after he was assassinated ... God, do you remember the day ... November twenty second, nineteen-sixty-three ..." She said it dreamily, as if it held some terribly personal meaning for her. Perhaps it did. It does for a lot of us.

"Yep, good old Cape Canaveral. Why not? That's where all the rockets take off from, isn't it? A girl wants to be in the movies — she goes to Hollywood. If she's lured by Broadway, she heads for New York. I wanted into the space program, so I went where I thought the action was."

"I take it that not all went as you had planned?"

"That's a very funny understatement, Derek, very funny. No, it damn well did not go at all. I got nowhere. Couldn't get anyone to even listen to me — let alone take me seriously. The only thing at all I learned was that I'd have to apply to NASA in Washington, and probably I'd need a Senator or two sponsoring me — just like they do the guys that want to be cadets at West Point or somewhere.

"Well, of course my parents weren't rich any more'n yours — we lived on the same side of the tracks, remember, Derek?"

I remember all too well, the derision that I

suffered at the hands of some of the wealthier kids, many of whom were now up at my mansion sloshing up the Chivas Regal. I supposed that Aloice had suffered the same as a youngster, perhaps even worse. The lack of fine clothes, make-up and all the other expensive stuff important to maturing girls probably made her more acutely aware than I of our true circumstances back then.

"So, my money soon ran out, down in Florida. I started whoring. There wasn't anything else to do. Oh, at first I was a waitress in a hash-slinging joint at thirty bucks a week, but the tips came only with a fat feel on the butt, you know? Then one night a guy offered me fifty bucks — *fifty bucks* — for a fast lay, so I did it. And after that, well ..."

"So what? I mean, nobody here knows that, you don't have anything to worry about."

"They do now. Or at least Chad does. Last night. He paid me. An ungodly large sum. He came up to me late and said he'd been talking to Myron, well, it's Myra Jenkins, now. About his or her sex change operation, and had decided to go ahead and himself, Chad, I mean, become a female. And ... he said he wanted one last really good bang from an expert.

"Well, I got as little girl indignant about that remark as I could — you sort of forget all those false ploys after you've been on the streets as long as I have, ya know? But he said he knew a whore when he saw one, that he'd pay twice my going rate for it, and whipped out a hundred dollar bill. Real crisp and new. I decided why not. Everybody was asleep and nobody'd know. Maybe he did deserve one last fling as a man — and I'm pretty good at my job, I'll have you know ..."

She spoke proudly, like a little homemaker who's been told repeatedly how good her apple pies are. "And besides, frankly I could use the C-note. This trip was pretty expensive, but I really wanted to come and I'm glad I did irregardless of everything that's happened."

I was thinking that in the final draft I could strike the erroneous 'ir' there since there is no such word as 'irregardless,' but she broke into my thoughts with, "I'll tell you one thing though, and this is strictly from professional experience, because in nearly twenty years, I've had about every kind of guy imaginable, I guess ..."

"What's that?"

"Chad Carter is no fag. Never was — never will be."

I pondered that for a moment, but didn't get too far because Aloice's hand was — getting too far — up my thigh, that is.

"Derek, if you didn't know about me — would you suspect? I mean, I've really tried to take care of myself ... see?" She slipped her elasticized bodice of her dress down to reveal a very respectable braless bosom, indeed. "Maybe you and I could ... here ... or at your cottage, if you like — not for money or anything, just for old times sake."

Well now, let me tell you something. A man, alone with a very desirable, albeit somewhat shopworn lady, who has just said, 'Hello, sailor — want a good time?' would no doubt be stupid not to take her up on the offer, without a second thought. But, I'm not just a plain ordinary man, alone with the decision, I'm a *writer*, and I've got who-knows-how-many of you breathing down my neck, wondering 'will he or won't he,' and thinking, 'well, we'll let him get away with a little dalliance now and then with certain 'nice' ladies — but with a *prostitute* ...?'

So I won't tell you what we did or didn't do. Except to say, we both returned to the mansion with pleased smiles on our pusses. Don't jump to any conclusions, because:

A. Aloice could just as well have been pleased to have me *not* take advantage of her generous offer, and further appreciate the gentlemanly way I declined, possibly with a brotherly kiss on the forehead.

B. What she had told me about Chad gave me enough brilliant clues in our pending murder case to put a happy face on any neo-gumshoe.

And 'C', ... oh hell, you're not my *wife*, you

know ...

When we returned, Burnside was in the midst of trying to re-enact the crimes — yep, just like in a B movie. There he had everybody gathered around the patio, and one by one he directed the players to their particular spot on the stage. It was really quite hilarious. He had the fat plumber, Donald Kirby by name, face down in the reflecting pool next to the one where Arbaugh's body had been found. It seems Kirby wasn't about to get into the one haunted by a dead man.

Anyway, he'd lie still for about ten seconds, and then start sputtering and complaining that he was going to drown. This looked all the funnier, because he had little black trunks on, and each time he rolled over and spouted water he looked just like a baby whale. Everyone gathered around, laughed and had a good time.

Then, Burnside had the three original body retrievers jumping around in the pool, and using Kareem's Nikon snaps for staging, the Lieutenant had the men position themselves properly around the little whale, who kept complaining about someone kicking his blubber. By then, the scene was hysterical with everyone yelling, laughing and splashing water.

The audience loved it — forgetting for the moment the macabre incident being disastrously recreated. Lydia Arbaugh had not forgotten however, and I arrived at the site just as she turned away, disgusted, running towards the sanctity of the house.

I followed and caught up with her inside. "Let's go have a drink in the library, Lydia. Those fools out there — they're just relieving tension. They don't mean any harm to you or to Paul's memory."

After she'd regained her composure and settled half way into a tall drink,I lighted my thinking pipe, the big burled curved job, and inquired of her, "This Justin fellow, what was his last name, do you remember?"

"Oh yes, it was Lamphere. Justin Lamphere."

"Lamphere ... sounds familiar, but that may just be because I know a reporter by that name over in Baltimore ... This Lamphere — Justin, I mean — you said he was from Oregon. Do you remember where exactly? Portland ...?" I was at a loss. "Geez ... there must be more than one city, let me check the Atlas .. okay, how about ... Eugene?"

"Yes. It was Eugene, Oregon."

Oh great! That'll save me from *actually* getting out of my chair and actually getting the Atlas down to try to lend some authenticity to this effort ... (if I'd been smarter, I would have just had Lydia say it was Portland in the first place, eh wot?)

"Okay, I'm going to do a little checking on his background — see if he can come up with anything that ties in with our current status quo. But, I can't

really do that until tomorrow, so how about a game
of chess — do you play?"

"Oh yes. It was Paul's favorite pastime when he
was working on a particularly aggravating problem."

"Flip for it?"

"No, I'll take black."

I opened with my famous king's knight sweep —
a very aggressive and virile opening gambit,
methinks, and sure enough, within fifteen minutes
the board was all but swept clean.

"Check!" I declared triumphantly.

"Mate." She replied smoothly.

I sat gazing at this latest abrupt fact of (my) life
— disbelieving that such a well thought-out
maneuver on my part could have been so devas-
tatingly thwarted. So fast. And expertly. And final.
And by such a pretty lady ...

"You can't win 'em all, chief." It was Kareem
entering the room in time to ease my embarrassment.

"Yes, uh, well, Lydia, Mr. Khan and I do have
some pressing matters to discuss, so ..."

Lydia arose gracefully, and exited the winner's
circle, chuckling fiendishly as she closed the huge
door behind her.

"Opened with the king's knight sweep again,
eh?"

"Shut up! Let's get down to business here. I've

got some juicy tidbits for you, and I assume with that glint in your beady little eyes you've got something worthwhile yourself. Let's compare notes."

Which we did. The plot thickened, but too many parts of it were downright coagulated, and refused to blend with the rest. We went over our facts, and sprinkled them with a lot of guessing and occasional far-out 'what if?' or two, but we seemed to be always returning to the beginning without further enlightenment.

"I've got an idea, Kareem — let's work this bassackwards."

"Howzzat?"

"Well, instead of concentrating on what seems to be factual and makes sense, let's ignore that and work on the stuff that *doesn't* fit. I'll reel it off and you make notes, okay?"

"Go ahead."

"Well, first of all we've got Chad as a homosexual by discovery — just like Lydia beat me at chess by a check by discovery. Things looked to be one way and were accepted on the basis of limited data, but were suddenly altered when yet another fact or two were added to the mix. In the case of Chad, all of a sudden he's not really a queer at all. I realize that gays have, in recent years, busted their closet doors and now it's fashionable for them to flaunt their perversion — but as far as I know, it is not yet the in-thing for a heterosexual to pretend to be a homo, unless it's for fun or profit. So make a note — I've got to talk to Myra Jenkins — see if he/she/it talked to Chad like he claimed to Aloice."

"He shit?"

"Huh? No! He, she, or it, I said. Just put down, 'talk to Myra.' Okay ... that brings us to Chad's boyfriend — Robert whatever. Make a note: 'check on Robert.'

"Next, we got this Justin fellow, Arbaugh's erstwhile helper on the electric car. His last name is Lamphere according to Lydia. From Eugene, Oregon. I don't see where he could personally have anything to do with the murders since he's dead, himself. That's why he qualifies for this little bastard list. Put him down — we'll check him out, too.

"The bald-headed fellow, Clarence Hildahl. I finally remembered him. He used to beat me up all the time in third or fourth grade. That's probably why I've forgotten him, mental block or something. Whatever ... he's from Saudi Arabia. Oil and all those mega-bucks. Just too pat. Too obvious. You say that your sources claim he does work for some oil outfit there, right? But what did you say he does?"

"He's a geologist."

"What would they need a geologist for over there — I thought the black stuff practically flows from kitchen faucents — I didn't think they had to actually go looking for it. I thought their only concern was how often they can get away with doubling the world market price for the stuff. Well, let's keep Hildahl in mind. Put him under 'butler did it.'

"Say, by the way, Phyllis showed me a wire awhile ago from my first wife, Jennifer. She had planned to be here for the reunion, and was in fact all set to go at the airport, but no one bothered to tell her United's on strike again, so she couldn't come ... too bad, might have been interesting to see the old bat. She's remarried three or four times since the divorce."

"So?"

"So, nothing. I mentiond her earlier in the story, and thought it might be nice to tie up her particular loose end now, rather than wait 'til later when, I dare say, we'll be running around this script like a one-armed paper hanger, trying to gather all the other loose ends."

"Makes sense."

"Well or course it does, although I'm sure there will be those who, upon hearing the original mention of Jennifer, thought it held provocative promise in store. If so, they are probably now disappointed — especially any of my old real-life wives, but geez ... I'm just not in the mood to cover any of that old tramped-thin ground, you know?

Besides, we can always revive Jennifer's character in some future epistle. Since I've more or less decided to make a career out of this series, I imagine that eventually we'll need every possible hook we can find, eh wot?"

"No doubt. By the way ... would you mind soft-pedaling that 'eh wot?' just a little — it gets sort of sickeningly repetitious after awhile."

"Okay — *okay!* It's just sort of a natural tag that slips out of the Selectric now and again ... well then, is there anything else we can do right now, or shall we see about dinner? Most of the group is back for our parting soiree, so we may as well make the best of it."

By eight that evening, most all of the original guests had assembled in the ballroom, with only a handful of Saturday's crowd having left early to return to their respective homes around the country.

As I entered the ballroom I thought to myself that this was the sort of thing the place must have originally been designed for. All the nattily dressed gentlemen and their ladies sporting the latest offerings of Yves Saint Laurent, Diane Von Furstenberg and J. C. Pennée. Everyone seemingly having a gay old time — especially Chad and Robert.

I spotted Lydia off to one corner being so-sorried to tears by the Pascale twins, and I went over to rescue her and ask if she'd be my dinner partner.

She replied that she'd be delighted, and I could almost hear the fluttering of a flirtatious hand-held fan of another era.

Dinner went smoothly, with Serenity in charge and Carlita seeming to get a big buzz out of scampering around from guest to guest — popping little tidbits of goodies into their mouths, rather than sitting down and enjoying the affair with the rest of the guests.

A round of toasts were made after dinner, led off by Artie Younger, who said, "May we all have another twenty years as good as the last, without all the bad stuff of course, like assassinations, Vietnam, Watergate, Nixon ..."

"Shut up and drink, Artie ..."

There were other, more somber and thoughtful toasts, and finally I arose and said, "Well, I see there's just about enough booze left to make one last solid and for-real toast, so here 'tis; May all of you who leave us tonight, go back to your homes, jobs and families with a renewed sense of the genuine camaraderie we've shared during the positive part of our reunion ... and to those of you who must remain with us until the good Lieutenant Percy A. Burnside turns you loose, I would again remind you; Please don't pee in the pool, or do anything perverted on the beds before removing the covers. Salute!"

Later, there was a lot of kissing and hugging,

plus the usual lies and promises to write, visit, phone or whatever that would never take place. Then the place was emptied, except for the twenty nine suspects, the police, the servants and the other little group consisting of Phyllis, Serenity, Kareem and myself. And Artie Younger, who insisted on staying until everyone was exonerated. His theory was that some mad killer, an escaped lunatic, was roaming the wilds of Virginia, and would soon be netted and all would be well.

Phyllis had cancelled her Monday morning flight, and would stay to offer support to Carlita, who seemed quite buoyant on her own. In fact, considering that she was one of the suspects, at least in theory, as she was the last person known to have seen Arbaugh alive, she seemed in no way unduly upset, and showed no sign of being perturbed at the oft repeated questioning by all of the officers at one time or another. I rather suspected she was enjoying the attention.

It was well after midnight when the place had cleared of the major throng, and the rest of us were sitting around drinking, talking and enjoying scraps of others' conversation when, for some reason, I stood up and said loudly for all to hear, "I am quite certain I have figured out who murdered Paul Arbaugh." Kareem looked at me as if to say, "You have exceeded your two drink limit, Mr. Dax, better go to beddy-bye," but I stood firm. "I am

currently assembling a few stray facts together
in my mind, and by morning, if we could all
reassemble here for breakfast at say, eight o'clock
— I will reveal the identify of the murderer." And
with that, I made as grand an exit as possible,
considering I had indeed, exceeded my two drink
limit by about four. Or five. Or ...

At the door, Burnside caught my arm and
demanded, "What the hell are you talking about,
Dax? If you know who the killer is, you'd better tell
me right now — or I'll have you for withholding
evidence. I wanna get this thing over and get out of
this circus — I got a wife and kids, ya know?"

"Sorry, can't help you right now, Percy. Wife and
kiddies will have to wait until breakfast. Night."

Before retiring, I found Phyllis, got her to dig
out her list of attendees, looked it over whilst she
looked me over like a duck stalking a June bug,
respectfully declined her offer to tuck me in, with a
"Thanks Phyllis, but I've got some studying to do.
Maybe tomorrow night — you'll still be here then."
That seemed to pacify her, and I then summoned
Kareem, and told him of my plan. He thought it
stupid or dangerous depending on how it turned out.
In the meantime, he promised to find Chad and ask
a couple pertinent questions we needed answered.

11

My idea was no big deal. Really. I just figured that if the killer was in our midst, if I blatantly indicated that I knew who it was, he or she would no doubt take steps to ensure my not revealing the fact at breakfast. Or, the killer might just think I was drunk (mostly true) and was making a blustering fool of myself, by grandstanding before the assemblage. That too, was partly the case.

About forty-five minutes after I'd gone to my room and thence fallen immediately asleep contrary to my original plan, I had the beejeebers scared out of me when suddenly I awakened to see a shadowy figure standing next to my bed, poised and ready to hit me with some solid information. "Pssst, it's me, Mr. Dax. Kareem."

"Oh, of course. I just dozed off a tad, apparently."

"You said you'd stay awake. Where's the gun?"

I looked around, but couldn't find a gun. Kareem panicked, something he rarely does, unless he holds

private panic sessions in his room that I know
nothing of. "The killer's got your gun — he'll kill
someone else, and you'll be blamed for it!"

"No. No. No. In the first place, it's *your* gun — I
don't own one, remember? And besides, it's right
here under my pillow."

"Oh."

"Well, did you grill our friend, Chad?"

"I didn't get a chance to really go after him, but I
did get Robert's, his lover's, last name. Your suspi-
cions were right."

"Well, what is it? How's anybody going to be
able to add it to their ditty bag of clues if you just sit
there with that stupid grin on your face?"

"Oh, well I didn't know you were ready to let
them know ... Lamphere. Robert Lamphere."

"Okay. I'm going to sleep. See you at breakfast."
I rolled over and shut my eyes. I never heard
Kareem say his customary nighty-night, because
he didn't. As I later learned, when he felt the pistol
butt tap him on the back of his skull, he merely
turned around to see if he could slap the offending
mosquito, but in so doing, his jaw was squarely
dealt a blow that knocked him flat. The last time that
happened, in Atlanta, as I recall, he was out for some
five minutes or more, so I now knew that he would be
of little value to me in my current plight, which in
the main could be summed up by the fact of my
looking down the barrel of a very large pistol, held

by none other than,

"Robert Lamphere! Well see, the trick worked. You took the bait downstairs, didn't you. Well, may as well put the gun down, ahem, the police, old Percy and his troops will be here any minute ... I said, you may as well put down the gun ..."

"I don't think so. I'm no dummy — and I'm no God damned fag, by the way, although that bit of info won't make no nevermind to you much longer, Dax."

"My, my — is that a threat?" Jesus, I hoped I wouldn't wet my pants like I did once before in a similar, highly stressful situation.

"No, just a fact. But first, we're going to get out of here. Come on, get up and don't try any cute moves."

I was glad that I'd kept my clothes on when I lay down on the bed earlier. I'd hate to be in my pajamas now for any number of reasons, not the least of which is that it's difficult to maintain a state of machismo in blue and white polka dots, and besides, if this guy did succeed in killing me, it's a hell of a way to go — in your jammies — Steve Martin's little song about King Tut going out that way, notwithstanding.

Like everyone else, I suppose, I've occasionally pondered the possible variables existant at the time of my demise, and by the process of elimination ruled out certain conditions I'd rather not see prevail at that auspicious moment. Like, I don't want to die on a bright sunny day. Just not a nice way to spoil it. It should be raining, cold and miserable. But the daytime is good — nighttime is too macabre.

Now, for the method. Well, right away I can give you a whole bunch of no-no's — such as the guillotine. Gad, what a mess! Or hanging, an automobile accident or any such smash-'em up device, or some lingering debilitating disease. Or a knifing — that's not a very pleasant prospect either, is it?

A heart attack. Good old, knock-the-socks-off heart attack. My father, grandfather and most every other relation in my immediate heritage checked out with a heart attack. Except cousin Marvin — he blew his head off. Talk about messy ...

Oh yes. I don't want it in bed, either — despite the old joke about, "heh, heh, heh, now *that's* the way to go!" Nope. Sitting in a chair, either reading or writing (I'll leave the specific choice to whomever punches the terminate button), but fully clothed, thank you — no damn pee-jammies!

During the foregoing reverie, Robert Lamphere hustled me out of the still and darkened house through the garden and towards the garage. I made one magnanimous gesture towards wresting the gun away from him as we entered the garage. My cleverly conceived plan was to slam the door on his gun arm just as we were passing through the doorway, but instead, I caught three of my own fingers and almost broke them off.

I didn't even have the pleasure of his realizing I was attempting to foil him, as after I'd yelled, "Ouch!" he merely inquired, "Whatzamatter, stub your toe?"

"Yeah, it's hard to see in the dark — I'll just turn a light on so we can see ..."

"Like hell you will! Leave it off!"

My eyes were fairly well adjusted to the minimal amount of light coming through the small window, the same one where two years before Kareem had almost gotten his big rump caught whilst we were prowling through our first caper, as he fondly calls these literary madnesses.

"Well, where do you want it?"

"I beg your pardon! You expect me to select a vital organ of my choice for you to insert a bullet? Very generous of you, Lamphere, but I was just rehashing some old thoughts about death and dying on the way down here, and I can assure you that being blasted away by a gun has low priority."

"Naw, I'm not going to shoot you."

I felt relieved to hear that, and relaxed a tad.

"I'm going to gas you, like Tucker. So, pick a car. Hell, you've got a dozen or so in here — must be a favorite or two."

"Yeah, there are fifteen very fine automobiles, to be exact. Twelve of my own, two of Kareem's —

that's his Mazerati over there ... and the white forty-nine Ford convertible ... that's his."

"Shit, I don't want a museum tour! Just pick a car!"

"... and the grayish blue Lotus on the end. That belongs to a dear old friend. Let's make it that one, shall we?" I was getting downright giddy — something I could afford, since none of this could possibly be happening for real — after all, I was in the middle of writing a book for God's sake (plus my own ninety percent after my agents standard tithe take) — and no asshole in his right mind is going to punch my terminate button now ...

We got over to the Lotus, but it was locked. I started for the keys board, but he stopped me and said, "You know, for what it's worth, I didn't kill Tucker. Just Arbaugh."

"Oh sure, hey, listen — what difference does it make — one murder, two murders, three — although I think that's supposed to be *your* line after I try to talk you out of this dastardly deed."

"No, I'm serious — I didn't kill Tucker." He acted like it was important to him that I believe him.

"Listen, I don't suppose I could talk you out of this, but unless you've got a pressing schedule, how about cluing me in on this whole deal. I mean, I have been racking my brain over this thing, and so far all I've come up with is this: You're related to Justin Lamphere, right? His brother?"

"First cousin. Father's side."

"Okay. He told you about the car, I assume, and you ..."

"Car? What car?"

"Hmmm? Oh, nothing. See, my mind wanders each time I face impending death by asphyxiation ... tell me then, it wasn't you calling the Arbaugh's house, making threatening remarks?"

"Hell no. What do you think I am, a pre-vert? I told you I wasn't no fag, and I can prove it." He fumbled for his billfold and said, "You got a match? I don't smoke, myself."

I fiddled around in my pockets and found my gold Colibri, the last present Felicia ever gave me. As I clicked it to life, I said out loud, "Felicia, I may be coming to visit you and Melissa any minute now — this may be the big one ..."

"What the hell are you talkin' about, mister?"

"Oh, just my wife and daughter. They were killed a couple years ago. That big plane crash in Chicago."

"Oh yeah, I remember. Sorry, but maybe you can understand then, how I felt when they took my son away ... here ... see, that's a picture of him when he was just about three. He's about twice that now. Isn't he a cute one?"

"Yes, he is. What's his name?"

"Daniel. Daniel David Lamphere."

A chill went up my spine. I was beginning to see

this whole thing a bit differently. "You mean...
Daniel David *Arbaugh.*"

The anger was unmistakeable in his voice.
"Yeah, shit. That's what *they* call him, but it's
Daniel David *Lamphere.* Always will be, to me."

"Listen, I'm shot ... if you'll pardon the
expression. Do you mind if we sit down in the Lotus
for awhile. I mean, that's where you'll want me
eventually anyway, for the, uh ... final curtain, as it
were?"

"Okay. Why not. I'm in no hurry, and I'm sure
you're not neither."

"Right." I unlocked the passenger door, and
then walked to the driver's side and he assured me
that his gun would be trained on me all the way. I
settled back into the bucket, reliving the brief but
pleasant times I'd had in the machine. "So, tell me
about it, Robert. Lots of gaps to fill in ... take your
time."

"Well, my cousin, Justin, was good friends with
Arbaugh from years back. When my wife and I
busted up, the kid sort of went up for grabs. I was in
jail for a couple things, and my damn bitch of a wife
took it all out on the kid. Beat him a lot. So, the state
took him away. Somehow, I think for money, but
Justin denied it, he fixed it up so Arbaugh and his
missus could adopt Daniel. Legal-like and everything.

"Later on, when I got out of jail, I beat the piss

out of Justin one day when I caught up with him in Frisco, and made him tell me where my kid was. But then I got picked up there, and put in the slammer for something else — just a little liquor store mis-understanding. That's where I met Carter."

"Chad?"

"Yeah."

"Tell me — is he a ...?"

"Fag? Naw. He does a female impersonatin' act at one of the dives out there — but no, he's straight. But he rolled some drunk fag that come onto him, and got caught and put in there with me for a spell."

"You mean to tell me that you literally met Chad Carter by coincidence, I mean both he and Paul Arbaugh were classmates, after all. That sounds a bit far-fetched, wouldn't you say?"

"I don't know about that, but that's the way it was. I went to Frisco to find Justin, did, then got thrown into the can and met Carter. Ain't my fault who he went to school with."

My head ached. This was a crucial part of my plotline, yet it seemed so incredulous. But then... many things in life are. I best not mess around with the truth, and just leave it the way it was. "So, how did all *this* come about?" I was getting restless to hear the story, if not the post script.

"Simple. Chad and me talked a lot — there's not much else to do in there unless you *are* queer, and it turns out he's a former classmate to Arbaugh. He says he's been invited to this reunion, although at the time he didn't know where it was gonna be, and I tell him I'd like to go, but he says no-can-do, only class members and spouses. Then, I get the swishy couple idea, but he says, no, he wants to be straight around his old buddies, and I suggest if he wants to be alive around his old buddies he'll agree to do it, which he does."

"But why all the bother — why not just go visit the Arbaughs in St. Louis, if you wanted to see them so badly."

"Well, for starters, I knew cousin Justin was there for some reason, probably to warn them or maybe to suck some more money from them for settin' up the adoption deal for Daniel. Anyway, although I've been able to best him a couple times, he's a mean bastard if he gets the chance, and I figured he'd just be itchin' to get his hands on me after Frisco, so I decided on this other way."

"Yes, but how did you know that Arbaugh would even go to the reunion — a lot of our fellow classmates didn't, you know."

"Carter talked to that Phyllis woman and a whole bunch of others at the same time — some sort of conference call, I think it's called. Anyway, Arbaugh was one of 'em who was on the phone and he said he and his wife were definitely gonna go."

"You went through this whole charade with Chad,and came all the way across the country to kill

Arbaugh, then?"

"Kill him? Hell no! I wanted to see him and talk him into letting me have Daniel back now that I'm out of the can, and back on the straight and narrow. I talked with him right off the first chance I got alone with him after Chad pointed him out to me. But he'd have none of it. He acted almost like I wasn't even there talking to him. Like his mind was somewhere else. Maybe he was doped up or something. But I sure as hell couldn't make him listen to reason.

"Then the other night after he was inside there with you guys at the party, he came out and I tried talkin' to him again, but he just ignored me, said something about his son being his son as long as he was alive to see to it, so I figured the only thing I could do was make certain he wasn't alive no longer — which I did. I slipped him the shiv, and he stumbled around for awhile and dropped in the pool. You know the rest."

"I wish I did. And you say that you did not kill Ernie Tucker out here in my forty-seven Caddie?"

"Hell no. Why would I do that? I didn't even know him."

"Well, why are you now so hell-bent on killing me out here — like whoever did kill Ernie?"

"Well, I figure the odds are on my side that the police will add your death to Tucker's, and come up with two of one kind against one of the other kind. And whenever they figure out who killed Tucker, they'll figure he also killed you, and ..."

"Arbaugh. Say, that's not all that ridiculous, Robert."

"You can call me Bob."

"Right. So what now?" Why did I ask that?

"Well, you know the answer to that one. I'm really kinda sorry about this, 'cause I don't see where you're all that bad a guy — even though you're rich and all. But well, you know all about me, and ..." he stiffened, and changed his voice to a command, "... start the engine. I won't konk ya out if you'll promise to sit here real quiet like. I'll get out of here in a second, and it won't take long for ya — I understand it's really painless ..."

"Oh, I'm sure it is. Say, why don't you join me in this little drive ... just to listen to the beautiful throaty purr of that eager engine — isn't it marvelous ...?"

"Yeah, well I'd better ..."

"Oh no! Sit back, listen to that sensuous purr ... but boy! When this thing takes off, it *really* motates ...!" I shoved the gearshift into low, slipped the clutch and whomped that baby to the floorboard. The Lotus lurched forward, pausing just long enough at the solid oak garage doors to completely mess up the snoot of Penelope's pride and joy. All this unexpected action had totally diskumboobled poor Robert, but he was starting to point the gun at me, and I doubted that this time I could slow-talk

him out of what he had in mind, so in desperation I
swung the steering wheel to a hard right, and threw
my body against his, all in one fell swoop.

Before either of us really was aware of what
was happening, the Lotus was whipping around the
garage at a sharp radius, and I felt the right side of
the car scraping the corner of the building, and then
a peculiar sensation of floating ... the contrast very
pleasant ... as if we were experiencing a stop-action
sequence in a movie. But then I saw and felt water,
and realized we'd plopped the Lotus and ourselves
in the ce-ment pond.

"I can't swim! I can't swim!" Lamphere was
screaming hysterically. His left arm was flailing
about, tearing at my face and right shoulder. I
noticed the gun still in his right hand, but it just sort
of dangled there. The underwater lights of the pool
illuminated the interior of the car, in a surrealistic,
ghastly fashion.

"Now that you mention it, neither can I swim, so
why don't we bail out before the water gets any
higher in here ..." I opened the door with ease,
expecting it to be difficult or impossible to open,
after all those horror stories I'd heard of people
being trapped in submerged automobiles. I didn't
know exactly where the Lotus had come to rest, but I
could see the slope of the pool floor, and therefore I
knew in which direction to head.

It's true, I can't swim, but I didn't panic as I was

fairly familiar with my surroundings, and knew I'd
need only force myself a few yards more to be in
shallow water. For a few moments the thought
crossed my mind that perhaps I shouldn't have
insisted on the double-size pool, because a normal
one would have me in safety by now.

I could feel Lamphere behind me, grabbing at
me and I tried to shake him loose, when I felt his arm
tighten around my waist, but I could not break free.
Suddenly, we shot to the surface and I lashed out to
slug him, and was fortunately able to pull that
punch at the last moment or I would have smashed
Kareem's glass jaw, and perhaps drowned him.

"Well, hello there, what kept you?"

Kareem laughed, blowing water out of his
mouth. "I think a Mack truck hit me in your
bedroom."

"Ah yes ... many a young lass has made a
similar comment ..."

We made our way to the side of the pool, and
Kareem tossed me out like a wet rag doll. I looked
around, but Kareem's feet, shoes and all, were just
disappearing below the surface.

Burnside's henchmen, followed a few paces
behind by Burnside, himself, were running towards
the pool. I shouted to them, "Hey, you guys!
Kareem's down in the pool looking for Lamphere.
Maybe you'd better help him."

Both of the lead fellows doffed their jackets and

shoes, and jumped in feet first just as Kareem surfaced with Lamphere in tow. He tossed the body on the deck, and jumped up next to it, and started resuscitation, but it was clear that Lamphere was dead.

"What in the hell is going on here?" Burnside had his service revolver out, and he was now trying to decide what to do with it, starting to put it back in its holster, then not sure if he should or not, and taking it back out.

"You can put that away, Lieutenant. I've seen enough guns for tonight."

"What happened to him?" Burnside wanted to know.

Kareem answered, having now given up trying to revive Lamphere. "He got his elbow caught in the door somehow, and couldn't get out and drowned."

"Must be when we hit the corner of the garage. I thought he was behind me in the pool, though, but it was you."

"Well, I'd sure appreciate your telling me about this in detail." Poor Percy was totally befuddled.

"Yeah, okay, Lieutenant. Let's go up to the house, first." As I left the pool area I glanced at the mess caused by the mishap, and suddenly realized that this was the first time I'd ever tried out the new pool. At least I was splashy about it. I overheard one of Burnside's men exclaim, "Christ, you'd better call the meat wagon, Al ... just tell 'em the Dax place —

they should know the address by now."

Indeed, they should. I only hoped it was their last trip for awhile.

When Kareem and I came down from changing into dry clothes, Carlita was scurrying around with a pot of hot coffee, and she prepared a cup for me, just as I like it, three fourths black brew, one quarter cold water. I hate blistering hot beverages of any kind. It's an insult to the lips, gullet and gut to ingest such boiling liquids — I leave that macho trip to all the truckers who've all but destroyed their innards anyway, with a variety of foreign invaders.

Burnside was naturally quite impatient to learn all the details of the latest escapade, and I obliged him with a full recount, starting with my boastful declaration earlier — the one where I announced that I would reveal the killer at breakfast. He allowed as how he'd heard that, since he was sitting at the table at the time, and further suggested that his opinion of that statement now, was unaltered from his opinion when he first heard it, "Stupid. Plain stupid."

"No doubt your comment, Lieutenant, is a valid one, but then again, my little speech did have the desired effect, didn't it ..."

After filling his little notebook with all the details of the incident, he wound down by asking, "Then, this Robert G. Lamphere, the most current addition to our deceased list, he confessed to you that he was the killer, right?"

"He most definitely did, and as I said earlier, he felt disposed to eliminate me, particularly in a method similar to Tucker's death, and I'm personally glad that he chose that method over the other options he had."

The questioning had taken nearly two hours, and some of the guests who had come down earlier to see what the commotion was all about, had returned for a few more hours of sleep. Only Lydia Arbaugh, Artie Younger, Phyllis Lindell, Clarence Hildahl, Kareem, Serenity, Carlita, Burnside and one of his assistants remained.

"Well, that about wraps it up for now, Mr. Dax. I think we can safely conclude that we have the killer of Arbaugh and Tucker. Tucker must have just been unfortunate enough to see Lamphere kill Arbaugh, so he got his mouth shut permanently."

"Yes, that would be a logical conclusion, Lieutenant." And indeed, it would be, given the information he'd gotten from me. Oh, I didn't lie. Everything I told him was truthful and factual. I just did not deign to give him all the details. How could I, when we still had another murderer in our midst — perhaps at this very table of stragglers — yet we had not a shred of proof to substantiate such an accusation.

The little gathering disbanded, most heading back to their beds to see if a delirious state of alpha sleep could be attained, before having to arise again, but Lydia purposely stayed behind, and as I suspected, it was because, "I'm ready for that cry now, Derek."

"Yes, I know. And there's only one proper place for it."

Silently, I took her hand and we walked outside the house, and strolled towards the cottage, as the sun started to dawn at our backs.

At the cottage, slender shafts of the new day's light pierced the darkness of the interior, and we had only entered the great room, and shut the door, when Lydia came to me. She embraced me in the timeless plea for understanding, comfort and strength, and I held her close, inhaling the fresh womanly fragrance of her lustrous raven hair. She sobbed but slightly, more perfunctorily than genuinely, but then this lady is not ordinary in any of her customs as she proceeded to prove by leading me to the bedroom.

As if in fulfillment of some sort of bargain we'd struck, she began to remove her clothes, methodically and carefully folding each garment neatly as removed, and stacking them in a precise little pile on a nearby chair.

Instinctively, I removed my turtleneck, but allowed the incredulity of the whole scene to stop the action. "Lydia ... are you sure you want ... so soon ... after ..."

But at the moment, she lowered the last item of attire, black lace bikini panties, and deftly stepped out of them, adding them to the rest of the stack of clothes. She then pulled back the covers, positioned her body on the bed in a manner that left no doubt that she thought it was none too soon. Her body was creamy smooth and white in the areas covered by yesterday's bikini at poolside. The rest of the body was lightly tanned. Perfect. Sensual. Inviting.

That peculiar sense of reasoning that has always seen me through questionable ventures came into play: "Who knows — we may all be dead tomorrow — why not enjoy life whilst we can?" So I did. We did. Over and over again. The woman had a voracious hunger, and the ability to stimulate my own insatiable taste buds.

Quite sometime later, she did cry — for real — and between sobs did a decent job of self depreca-tion, suggesting that perhaps it was perverted of her to want love and sex in the wake of her husband's death. I reassured her that the reaction is a totally normal one, since many humans harbor a deep seated correlation between sex and death even under the most normal circumstances. "Even when a friend or relative dies, it's not uncommon for a person to suddenly become inexplicably aroused sexually. After my father died, I got so horny my wife almost divorced me, but a girlfriend of hers, a psychiatrist, explained such a reaction is not abnormal. It doesn't happen to everyone certainly, but you shouldn't be ashamed if it does."

That professional dissertation seemed to assuage her and it surely made me feel less guilty, and she started to make serious negotiations towards another near-term rematch — but I noticed that it was almost seven-thirty, and suggested we join the others for breakfast.

Fastidious to the end, Lydia skillfully dissuaded me from showering with her, and by the time we'd taken turns at the bathroom, it was well after eight o'clock.

On the walk back, I told her that contrary to what I had led Burnside to believe, Lamphere did not kill Tucker. That didn't seem to either surprise or worry Lydia, and for a gut-piercing moment, I wondered if I had just spend several deliciously wanton hours in bed with a murderer. Pardon me, if she *was* the killer, she would insist on her due of the proper title ... murder*ess*.

12

"Well, if I didn't know better, I'd say where have you two lovebirds been roosting?" It was Artie Younger greeting us at the edge of the patio. I shot him a look that caused him to add, lamely, "... but then, of course, I do know better ..."

Lydia walked past him with an air of disdain, much as the Queen might pass the Royale Garbage Depository.

I indicated to Lydia that she should go on without me, and motioned for Artie to have a seat on the patio deck. "Tell me, Artie, have you kept in contact much with Ernie Tucker these past few years?"

His perpetual smile flagged momentarily, but returned with his reply, "Oh no. Not really. We both attended the other reunions. But other than that — no, we haven't seen or spoken to one another in the last five years. Why?"

"Well, I'm just trying to find someone who may shed some light on him or his circumstances —

anything that might cause somebody to want to murder him."

"Murder Ernie? Why, I thought that was all settled! That Lamphere character killed him because he saw him kill Arbaugh."

"No, that's what Burnside decided on his own. I didn't say that Lamphere confessed that to me." I purposely held Artie's eyes with my own for a too-long moment, but he did not react, only to smile and say, "Well, old Ernie didn't have any other enemies — not here, anyway. He was amongst friends tried and true, you know that, Derek. It had to be Lamphere that killed 'im."

Artie paused, not sure he wanted to ask the question that was bugging him. "Uh ... you said Lamphere didn't confess *to* killing Ernie, but ... did he say he *didn't* kill him ... I mean, specificially?"

"Yes." The affirmation all but slapped Artie across the face. "Well, we'd better get into breakfast — I made a big fool of myself last night, boasting that I'd announce the name of the killer this morning. I'd better get in there and do something about that ... coming, Artie?"

"No, well, yeah ... I'll be there in a minute. You go ahead ... at least, you can sure as hell tell everybody Lamphere killed Paul ..."

"Yeah, I can do that, *too.*"

I left Artie Younger sitting alone, looking very worried. I only wished I could figure the exact reason for his concern. But that was furnished by Kareem the minute I entered the dining room. He hailed me off to one side, and showed me some notes and elaborated on them with additional information he had secured only moments before by telephone.

"Okay, Kareem ... you'd better call old Percy back here ... no, leave him alone for now, we can get him later. Let's go eat."

Most everyone had eaten by the time I was seated, but I was ravenous after my early morning work-out so I sat down and gobbled up some eggs and ham, whilst the others lingered over coffee, and further discussed the main topic of the day ... and night.

"Derek, do you think the Lotus can be salvaged? It's such a beautiful car — even now, sitting down there in the water." It was Miriam Wilson, inquiring about the liquid death chamber. Funny how life's problems, decisions and small talk do go on no matter what. "Oh, the Martians landed yesterday and destroyed the entire west coast ... isn't that terrible... I guess that means Disneyland is out for this year ... and the children *so* looked forward to it ... oh, but then there's Disney*world* — how wonderful!"

"I imagine the Lotus can be dried out and put back together quite nicely. No hurry, it's owner won't need it for awhile." Which reminded me, speaking of life going on, I'd have to tell Penelope about her pride and joy's midnight meandering. Maybe I'd go

up to visit her sometime. Be a good excuse, although
I don't know why I feel that I should need one ...

"Okay, ladies and gents. Last night in my
slightly inebriated condition, I stated that at
breakfast I would announce the killer ... and to that
end, I hereby state that one Robert G. Lamphere is,
or was, the person responsible for murdering our
friend and former classmate, Paul Arbaugh."

The others quieted down, satisfied, their minds
already working on plane schedules, lists of items
to be remembered and packed.

"But we must not forget our other friend who
was murdered ... Ernie Tucker ... Oh, Artie, I'm glad
you could join us ... come sit down over here." I
motioned to a chair next to mine. "As I was
saying, we lost two good friends this weekend, plus
a spurious one, of course, in the person of Robert
Lamphere.

"But Lamphere did *not* kill Ernie — only Paul.
He told me so, and at the time, he had nothing to lose
or gain, so I believe he was telling the truth." My
little audience put down their mental packing list
and grew attentive.

"But who would kill Ernie, and why? He was so
nice and helpful." Carlita had stopped her rounds of
cup refilling to ask.

"Well, we have been working on that for the past
day and a half, Kareem and myself, and we have
concluded certain facts:

"First, someone for reasons known best to them, prevailed upon Ernie to switch their prophecy, replacing the original one with a modified version. We know that the bank explosion that killed Ernie's father did *not* damage the vault or safety deposit boxes at all. The building was totally destroyed, as were Ernie's father and his secretary who apparently lighted an after-glow cigarette — without realizing the gas main was leaking. But the contents of the safety deposit boxes were unharmed.

"Ernie used the fire as a convenient excuse to us for the wax seal being melted away. He probably also scorched the envelope a little — just for effect. Why he agreed to do this, we're not certain, but in addition to friendship, it may have been for money. Ernie's bank wasn't in the best financial shape. The local savings and loan, by law, has been able to offer a higher rate of interest on deposits, and last year Ernie lost many hundreds of thousands in deposits. Also, his wife recently left him, so I suspect if someone offered him a goodly sum to effect the prophecy switch, he might have been tempted.

"Naturally, we know the person whose prophecy was switched." I paused to allow each of those seated around the breakfast table to aim an accusing eyeball or two at their neighbor.

"Secondly, that same person was seen the night of the murder, by me, with wet pants legs, but he was not one of the fellows who assisted Doc Wilson here,

and the others in pulling Paul's body from the pool."
Again, I noticed several of the breakfast trade
sneaking glances at one another.

"We've done a little checking, and find that
person's personal and financial affairs to be in a bit
of dissarray, not unlike Ernie's — but on a more
serious scale. We suspect that something in that
original prophecy would have caused a worsening
of either his business or personal status, and it had
to be obliterated.

"Thirdly, Ernie's murder might have been an
afterthought. After Paul's death, we think the
perpetrator of the prophecy switch decided to kill
Ernie just as a precaution against his talking or
later demanding hush money — or perhaps Ernie
had already been blackmailing him — in any event,
his killing could be seen by the police as a tie-in with
Paul's, and when Paul's killer was discovered, no
doubt he would be charged with Ernie's death as
well. Thus, Ernie's true murderer would be
permanently off the hook.

"Fourthly, as promised last night, I will now
reveal the killer — the second killer — who is
amongst us now, at this very table, and none other
than our funny friend ..."

"Artie! It's Artie Younger!" After all that, Chad
Carter has to steal my punch line, but why is he
yelling Artie's name. Oh yes, it's because Artie is
standing there with a big gun pointed at ... *Phyllis?*

"All right, Goddammit, Dax. " I noticed Artie wasn't smiling. At all. "You've figured out a lot of shit, but it's really funny, because you're way off base on most points, but the way you and the big ape with the silly voice are going at it, you may actually get around to the truth, and I'm not about to have my balls strung up for this — not when it was all really Phyllis' fault in the first place!"

Kareem claims that with training, you can stand before a man armed with a gun, and by watching his eyes closely, determine a split second before he pulls the trigger, when he's going to do it. The eyes flinch just a tad. If you have lightening-fast reflexes, you then only need to move out of the way of the bullet. Claims he knew a guy in Paris once whose very successful stage act consisted of doing that very thing — dodging bullets fired from guns fired at him from audience volunteers. "What happened to your friend?" "One day he got a guy from the audience who didn't flinch."

Kareem's own reflexes must be slowing down just a tad, because as he was yelling "Geranimo!" and sailing through the air with his devastating 'Pakistani Parachutist Karate' move, Artie was pulling the trigger of his gun which was still aimed at Phyllis. But he only got off one shot, because by then he had two number twelves doing a body press on his chest.

Doc Wilson didn't know where to place his

allegiance, so I yelled, "Get to Phyllis — Kareem usually mops up after his own victims." And that's just what Kareem was doing almost as soon as he got off the floor and had dusted himself off.

"Oh, I really messed him up ... five, maybe six ribs broken." He slapped Artie's face to revive him, and in time he did come around, moaning and in great pain — trying to regain some of the air that had been stolen away.

Meanwhile, Doc Wilson pronounced Phyllis in fine shape, except for a small graze wound on her upper left arm. I gave Carlita Burnside's card and asked her to call him, and to bring an ambulance.

Whilst he awaited the return of the troops, Artie and Phyllis verbally abused each other, until at last, I suggested that since Phyllis seemed in better condition to talk, perhaps it would be nice of her to add the remaining brush strokes to our incomplete portrait of murder. (Yes, I agree that is rather syrupy — but let's leave it in — makes me sound like a well-rounded writer, methinks.)

Phyllis seemed only too anxious to oblige, much like a person eager to purge the contents of his stomach in the toilet bowl once it becomes obvious it's not going to exit through proper channels.

"It all goes back. Way back. When we went to Washington on the senior trip, I was already pregnant. I didn't know it then, but I was. By Artie. When I found out, I went to him, but he said he'd go to jail first before he'd marry a slut like me. Those were his exact words. He said he could prove that I'd slept around with other guys — he'd just have to get you, Derek, and the others who had such a fun time with me at the Tidal Basin — to testify to that.

"I was distraught — back then, a girl didn't get an abortion as easily as nowadays, and I tried to kill myself. I ended up in the hospital, instead, and met a real nice older boy there. Fred. He was an orderly, and came by several times each day just to cheer me up. Well, he only had to ask me once to marry him, considering my condition.

"We had quite a few good years together, Fred and me. He loved me, and in a way I loved him — for what he did for me when no one else — Artie, that bastard over there — would.

"Well, a couple years ago, when Fred and I were starting to have some marital problems — mostly over Lizzie — that's my oldest daughter, Artie's daughter, by biological fact — well, she was kind of wild like I was at her age, running around with boys, stayin' out late, you know ... Well, I was wrong and Fred was right, because by letting her have too much freedom — just the opposite of the way I was brought up — Lizzie got pregnant. But at least the boy that got her that way was decent enough to marry her.

"That's how I got to be a grandmother at thirty-seven." There was a touch of unique pride in

Phyllis' voice. After all, regardless everything else, she could in fact claim the singular accomplishment of being the first of any of us to become a grandparent. "Anyway, Fred and I, like I say, had some bad times over all that, and somehow I sort of got hooked up with Ernie Tucker. I'd done all the banking for my family for years — Fred didn't have any knowhow when it comes to managing money — and I saw Ernie once or twice every week, because of that.

He just has ... had ... a real small bank. Just him and two or three tellers. Ernie was getting divorced, and having some bad trouble at the bank — just like you said, Derek — and well, in the middle of all that we decided to try and get rid of our troubles — his wife and my Fred — and make the best of things together. Just Ernie and me.

"But that would take some money. I had figured out once that if I'd gone to court and got support monies for Lizzie from Artie, over eighteen years — that's how long he would have had to legally pay me — that would amount to over a hundred thousand dollars with interest.

"So, I called Artie and asked him for that much. I knew he was doing just fine, 'cause he was braggin' all over the place at the last reunion five years ago. But he refused, said he was having some cash flow problems or something, and also that he was having marriage problems of his own. Ruth, his wife, watched every penny and if they got divorced she was already going to get at least half of everything as it was.

"Well, Ernie and I were desperate — so I kept calling Artie every now and then, and finally I told him if he didn't pay up for his daughter I'd raised for him, I'd go to Ruth and tell her all about it, plus the fact Artie was a grandfather as well. I told him I bet if she knew all that he'd probably have to pay much more than the hundred thousand I was asking for — which I felt, and still do, was rightfully mine.

"Well, finally Artie agreed. I had told him in one of our conversations about Ernie and me, 'cause we didn't have anything to lose by Artie knowing, and Artie said, okay, he'd raise the money somehow, but there was the matter of that stupid class prophecy thing that Ernie was keeping, and part of the deal was that Artie'd get to see it, by himself, before he'd give us the money."

I interrupted her fascinating dissertation with, "Then Ernie had not, as he told us the other night, had not peeked into the package?"

"Oh no. He would not have betrayed the confidence of the class. No, the package was still sealed with the original wax do-hickey. But anyway, now that we had the chance to get the money, and it seemed to hinge on that old prophecy thing, Ernie and I figured why not — *what* difference would a thing like that from nearly twenty years back make.

So, when Artie brought the money, he sat in the private little place Ernie has at his bank for people wanting to look in their safety deposit boxes. Artie was in there quite awhile, and when he came out, he gave me the hundred thousand dollars and left.

"I never saw or talked to him again until I got accidentally appointed secretary, by default, of this shindig after Mary Perkins killed herself." Phyllis seemed to feel she'd said her piece, and smiled at Carlita who offered a cup of tea.

"Okay, Phyllis. Fine. But what about Ernie?"

"She killed him! She killed the poor miserable bastard!" Artie started to get up as he shouted, but the pain of the effort drove him back to the carpet.

Phyllis hesitated for a moment, but seemed to bask in the limelight and continued, "Well, we got Artie's money like I told you. Everything was just fine. There was the reunion coming up, and we looked forward to being with each other here, away from all the old people and places at home, you know? I was really excited, and thought Ernie was, too. But when he got here, he told me that he and Betsy — that's his wife — were talking about getting back together, and that he was using the trip to get away from everything and think about it.

"He said later, Saturday night, just before the party started, that he had thought about it, and that's what he was going to do. Go back with Betsy. But also, he said he needed the hundred thousand — all of it, and said if I went back with Fred I'd be taken care of good enough that way — that I didn't need the money as badly as he did.

"I told him, no. That was my money, my pay for raising Artie's child, and Ernie didn't have any right to it unless I said so, but he reminded me the money was in his bank, and besides, most of it was already spent to cover something he'd screwed around with in the books. I insisted that he give me my money back, so then he threatened to tell Lizzie that Fred wasn't her real father, and tell that to anyone else in town if I didn't let him have the money scott free.

"Well, I was fit to be tied, but we went on with the party like nothing had happened, and then poor Paul ... got killed ... I used to like him in school — he was so much smarter than the rest of us, remember? Always knew all the answers — for real — he never cheated on tests or anything ...

"Anyway, during all the commotion after Paul's body was found, I got Ernie off near the garage to talk about our situation again. He pulled me inside the garage so no one would see us talking — always so conservative about everything — just like a banker.

"Anyway, as we talked, he kept wandering from car to car, saying how nice they all were. How he wished he had some like that.

Then he saw that old Cadillac convertible and went crazy. He ran over to it and said it was exactly like the one his daddy had years ago. He got in it, and just sat there like a little kid pretending he was driving. Made motor sounds and everything.

"I got in next to him and again asked him about my money. He got really nasty, the first time I ever saw him like that. 'Phyllis!' he yelled, real mean like, 'You can't have that money! I need it. Do you understand? I got to have it,' he yells, 'and if you give me any more static about it, I'll forclose on that damn mortgage of yours on the house. Your Fred's behind several months on the payments, anyway.'

"Then, he got just as calm as you please, like he hadn't said nothin' untowards at all, and said, 'Phyllis, get me the keys for this thing off the board over there — Derek told the other guys it was all right if we wanted to take one for a spin. Clarence told me.'

"I couldn't believe how he'd changed — real mean one second, then perfectly natural, like everything was fine and dandy the next. I went over and found the keys and I also found a big wrench, and went back to the car and hit him with it as hard as I could. He fell over and I put the keys in, had a devil of a time figuring out how to start it — it's not simple like modern cars. Then I left. I figured it was a fitting way for Ernie to die — in a Cadillac he liked so well.

"I was going to tell everyone what happened, in fact, I did tell Artie, but he said to keep quiet about it — even promised me some more money. So I didn't say any more to anybody else. By the way, that's when he fell into one of those little decorative pools and got his pants wet. Artie, I mean. Just plain fell in by accident. He didn't have anything to do with Paul's drowning, or whatever he died from."

"And that's it?"

"Yeah, Derek — that's all she wrote." Phyllis seemed relieved rather than repentant.

I glanced at Artie who himself, managed to look somewhat relieved, but that condition was to change abruptly. "But that isn't all, Phyllis. You didn't kill Ernie." I enjoyed the startled look on her face for a few moments. "Oh, you will be charged as an accessory, to be sure, but it was Artie who actually killed Ernie, after all. You see, he contrived to accidentally find Ernie's body in the running Caddy, with Clarence Hildahl and Victor Louden along as witnesses.

"But, when Artie started to pull Ernie out of the car, he noticed that Ernie was still breathing, so without the others noticing, he choked off what life was left. It didn't take much — Ernie's lungs were filled with carbon monoxide anyway, but Artie could have saved his life if he'd tried. He is trained in CPR and other emergency first aid. Morticians probably are as skilled in that regard as the average doctor.

"So, ladies and gentlemen, as I started to say earlier, and as was prominently billed last evening, I *now* give you our second killer ... Artie Younger. Phyllis here, is an unexpected bonus. Case closed, Kareem?"

"Acha!" (Good old Pakistani affirmation)

By evening, everyone had left, including the temporary staff which had cleaned up everything quite nicely, although not entirely to Carlita's liking as she was now scurrying about flicking bits of dust that had been missed, arranging pillows neatly on the couches, and so on.

Serenity watched Carlita busying herself and smiled. "Derek, she is a real gem. You should capture her, if you can." Which is what I did. Carlita jumped at the position offered her as 'Mansion Manager" as I pompously called it, and as Lydia, Kareem, Serenity, Carlita and I lifted our glasses in a toast to the new relationship, Kareem said, "Oh, I forgot, Serenity, the ... you know ..."

"Oh my yes, dear." And to the rest of us, "Excuse us, we'll be right back."

Lydia looked at me in mild amusement, but I could offer no reason for my two friend's scampering up the stairs like two children off to explore an attic. But soon the mystery was resolved, as Kareem and Serenity bounced down the stairway, each concealing something behind their backs.

"We wanted to give you these little house-warming gifts last night at the party, but we never quite got that far. Uh, Serenity, first you."

"Okay. Derek, as you know, in the publishing business, a publishing firm or most anything connected with it is called a 'house', right? And, well you're a writer, so there's *that* part. Then, you remember that old nursery rhyme about the house that Jack built? Well, it's stretching the whole idea a bit, but ..." She motioned to Kareem, who held up a huge bronze plaque engraved with the inscription, THE HOUSE THAT DAX BUILT.

"That's actually from me, for over the front door, but I couldn't lift it. But this one is from Kareem." Serenity produced a gilt-framed painting of Napoleon in full dress uniform astride a magnificent white mount.

"Why, that's terrific — you know of course, my keen interest in Napoleon, and ..." Then I caught the sneaky look in both Serenity and Kareem's eyes. I peered closer at the painting. In place of old Nappy's pudgy little puss, Kareem had painted mine — and for good measure had just the bowl of a pipe sticking out from a breast pocket. We all started to laugh — even Lydia, who appeared even more beautific as an alive, spirited human than as a sombre, doleful sophisticate.

We lifted a few glasses, and Carlita insisted on finding just the right place for the painting, and left us to commence that mission,

"Well, what will you do now, Lydia? I'd like to have you stay on here, if ..."

"Oh no, you're very kind, Derek, indeed, all of you have been just marvelous, but I'll have to fly back with Paul ... Paul's body, and make the funeral arrangements. And then there's Daniel. I'm anxious to get back to my son ..."

"Bring him here, Lydia. It's a great place to raise a child. Horses, wide open spaces, the tennis court ..."

"Oh, Derek, I know you mean that ... now ... but let's give it all some time, okay?" She leaned over to kiss me, oblivious to Kareem and Serenity's presence.

"Okay. As you say. But the offer's open. Listen, what about the car — Paul's invention?"

"I don't know. As I told you, he evidently disposed of it. I really don't know what he did. I think he didn't trust me to know, since before, when he wanted to destroy just the original idea, I forced him to continue."

"You haven't any idea what he could have done with the car?" Serenity joined the conversation. "Do you suppose he dismantled it, or hid it someplace?"

"I just simply do not know, Serenity. He was not really himself the last few weeks. He could have done most anything, I guess." She paused, thoughtfully. "One other thing I don't quite understand. What was so important about Arthur Younger's original prophecy that he wanted so desperately to replace it with the altered version?"

"We don't really know, Lydia. There were all sorts of possibilities that came to mind, something he might have written about one of the girls, about some perverted desires or about some master plan to take over the world. I don't know. Kareem and I racked our brains over that, and finally decided perhaps, it was just that he wanted to maintain his reputation as a funny man, and since he was in town to hand over the hundred thousand anyway, he just decided to maybe add some spice to whatever he'd originally written."

"Did you ask him why?"

"Oh yeah. But he said he'd take the reason and the original prophecy to his grave with him. I think he means it."

That night, Lydia offered me only a chaste kiss goodnight, and hurried to her own bedroom. No explanation. Nor was one really needed. I imagine she had had second thoughts about the propriety of our wild liaison earlier that day. So be it.

The next day, I delivered her to the airport and saw her off. We both said we'd write or phone. We both knew we would not.

They pulled the Lotus from the pool, and an hour or so later I started it up, and I swear the thing shook itself dry much like a sheep dog jumping out of a bathtub.

Kareem helped me get the damaged garage and the garden back in shape. We both enjoyed the physical labor, and it was a couple days later as we were patting ourselves on the back over the fine job we'd done, when a big semi truck blatted an announcement of its arrival. A cigar-chomping, stubby fellow jumped from the cab and demanded, "This here Derek Dax place, is it?"

"Yep. What you got there?"

"A damn little car. All the way from Saint Louie, Moe. Shit! Can't you find none like that around here?!"

"No ... I sincerely doubt it." I looked at Kareem conspiratorily and we both went to the rear of the truck.

"You guys are gonna have to help me roll off the little bastard. Says here it can't be drove. Something wrong with the transmission, I guess. The hood's all taped shut and the back end's filled with boxes."

We got the mustard-colored little beast out. Kareem picked up one end by himself after it was on the ground. Just to flex his muscles. Seeing that, the driver allowed as how he wouldn't mind having Kareem along to make deliveries. I thanked the guy, and he laboriously backed his big rig down the drive, trampling only a couple shrubs in the process.

I checked the manifest and noted that the date the car had been ordered out of storage and its transport to me consigned, 'By phone call authorization from owner, Paul J. Arbaugh,' was the Saturday of Paul's death. Probably after he and I had our brief meeting of minds.

As Kareem and I examined the car, it became clear that the empty boxes had been stuffed inside only to camoflage the huge generator and part of the batteries which were otherwise exposed.

"Well? Let's try it out!" I jumped in and Kareem got in the passenger's side, his weight tipping the thing severely. I turned the key, and off we went over hill and dale, smoothly, with only a barely audible whirring sound. When we came back to the garage area, we got out, untaped the hood, marveled over the ingenuity of the contraption, and I said to Kareem as I rubbed my face in thought, "What's the very basic thing that super-duper secret group of yours teaches?"

And he replied, pronouncing the word the only way he can, since despite his other accomplishments he has yet to master the proper pronounciation of a 'v', 'surwiwal.' "

"Yeah, that's what I figured. Okay, champ, let's get the shovels."

By dusk, we had it buried and were tamping down the loose earth. What else could we do.?

13

We started sort of a tradition in *"The Enchanted Cottage* by refusing to have a chapter thirteen, this, not because yours truly is superstitious, but because many readers are, and I see no reason to antagonize them.

It's really all kind of silly, you know — the morbid fear of triskaidekaphobia. Most commercial buildings number the floors in such a way as to eliminate floor thirteen. The numbered buttons in the elevators jump from twelve to fourteen. In my judgment, that little cover-up is futile, since a true triskaidekaphobic (wow — what a mouthful!) would see right through that simplistic ploy, and refuse to land on or proceed beyond the fourteenth floor, as obviously, it is really and truly the thirteenth.

You see my point.

In any event, since my first novel in this series was so exceedingly successful and well-received by the more erudite reading public, and in view of the fact that it did not contain a chapter thirteen, neither *this* book or any subsequent ones will have a chapter thirteen. Wouldn't want to mess with a good thing.

'course, like I say, *I'm* not superstitious ...

14

I had no intentions of seeing Lydia Arbaugh again. Our farewell scene at the airport fostered a finality that seemed to indicate that what we had had together was good, but also bizarre. Not something to be nurtured. 'It was just one of those crazy things' as the popular song used to blare out at us from the green-eyed Philco. Leave it alone. So I did. Well, for about two months, anyway.

During that period after the class reunion, I finished the novel I'd been working on, sent it off to the great bearded one who was vacationing in Jamaica per usual, and spent some time taking lessons from Kareem in self defense. The first time we had a go at that, I realized that Kareem does not take lightly such matters as life and death.

This formidable mixture of karate, judo and Asian mind control he's so expert at is no sport with him. It is deadly serious as hell, and even when he's just practicing the art, that fiercly piercing look comes into his eyes, and I should think that a genuine human target of that alone would say, 'Okay, fella, I give — turn off the laser beams!'

I cannot precisely describe all the inhuman things he taught me to do to another human being if ever my life were in peril, but one I recall vividly, because he didn't quite pull his punch, or perhaps I should say, pull his pull. That particular maneuver has to do with when you're seated and some shadowy figure approaches you with a gun and suggests that you get up and walk straight ahead and act normal, or whatever that tired old line is.

What you do, according to the gospel of Saint Kareem, is to reach out and grab the guy's testicles and yank 'em like a church bell. I can attest to the fact that such an action indeed evokes a reaction similar to a whole belfry full of clanging in one's head, because after telling me what he was going to do, he proceeded to do it — *to me* — not entirely faking the move, an unhappy fact to which I eluded earlier.

I literally ended up in the hospital, and cute little nurses popped in and out of the room for three days, just to see 'that rare disease called elephantitis.'

I did learn some important defensive gestures and even a few really offensive ones — in addition to the one already described, although in Kareem's opinion that simple(?) one comes under the heading of self-defense.

I also sort of learned to swim. I know it sounds ridiculous that a quasi-adventure hero like myself can't swim, what with Jimmy Bond and old Travis McGee jumping into the middle of oceans all the time to save a damsel in distress. But damsel, uh, dammit, I can't. Or couldn't. I could tell you something funny about that, and I guess I will ... nothing good on the tube tonight anyway.

Back when I was a kid, I was a Cub Scout, then a Boy Scout. Worked hard and got all the merit badges. I mean *all* of them. I had those multi-colored patches on my uniform, on my cap, and plastered clear around a special sash designed for that purpose. Had 'em all except one — the swimming merit badge. I especially needed that one to qualify for Eagle Scout ranking — the pinnacle of the scouting experience.

I'd had a close encounter of the drowning kind when, as a little kid, a ring I was wearing got caught on a nail protruding from a dock I was dog-paddling under, and had I not ripped free ...

So. Each time I tried to actually swim, the moment my feet left the bottom of the lake, river or pool — I tried them all — I'd panic. Finally, it got embarrassing with others around, so I prevailed upon my mother to cart me every day during the summer months to a secluded bluff overlooking a local lake, and she'd sit patiently, offering encouragement, as I tried in vain to get my feet — both of them — to come unglued from the murky bottom of Crotch Lake. No really — that's its name, Crotch Lake. It's still on the map — I checked.

Ultimately, I realized the whole attempt was futile, but I desperately wanted that one illusive merit badge, and moreover, I wanted the elite Eagle Scout status. There was only one other in our entire city, and he was our Scoutmaster, some ten years my senior.

The rules for qualifying for the swimming merit badge said, 'applicant must display ability to traverse water over his head in depth, for a distance not less than one hundred yards.' I looked up 'traverse' in the dictionary. Didn't say anything about swimming. But, wow! Three hundred feet! An entire football field — goal to goal! Impossible! Yet ...

I had gotten to know quite intimately my watery territory beneath the bluff where my mother dutifully watched her youngest son giving his all for the advancement of scouthood. I knew that about forty feet from shore the water was approximately six feet deep, and it remained that depth for another twenty feet or so before heading directly to China.

I got my scoutmaster, the lone Eagle Scout, to come out to Crotch lake for my public swimming debut. I paced off the hundred yards on the beach — even stuck a stick at each end. I thought he'd probably just sit back on the bluff and watch my performance, as my mother always did, but no, this guy was gung-ho all the way. He stripped to his scivvies and followed me all the way out to the deep section.

"Here I go!" I yelled. "See that first stick on the beach?" And off I went, parallel to the shore line, the upper part of my body executing a perfect Australian crawl, whilst the lower part of my torso bobbed up and down, courtesy of my feet urgently seeking, finding and bouncing off the lake bed.

I made it to the far stick. I passed the test. I got my swimming merit badge. I did not receive my dubious due as an Eagle Scout however, as the old lone eagle took off with his neighbor's wife before submitting the papers to headquarters — the papers which would initiate my award. It didn't matter much though, because by then I'd transferred my enthusiasm for scout pins to hairpins and all the delightful lovelies held together by same.

Kareem was about as patently amused by that stalling story as you probably are, and he promptly tossed my flailing body into the deep end of the pool, and then proceeded to step on my fingers each time I attempted to grip the coping.

Funny how fast you can acquire a new skill when the motivation is sufficiently intense ...

★ ★ ★ ★

After a few weeks, our little respite ended. My body was back in reasonably fine working order, and I started my fall tour of the mid and south west, giving lectures, hitting the talk show circuit, and all the other stuff writers must do to plug their wares. Don't you wish we could transport some of history's notable literary giants to our dimension in time? Imagine Willie Shakespeare on Merv's program, or Tolstoy on the Tonight Show. "And tonight's guests are Becky Jean Whynot, star of that new flick, *"Cheerleaders in Outer Space,"* Janey Smellea, from the zoo with a couple cute furry animals, and of course, Count Leo Tolstoy, who will regale us with a few of his pinko philosophies. I hear the Count has a new book, a big mother, what's it called ... staff? Oh yeah, *"Peace or War"* — something like that. Should be fun. Stay with us."

So there I was in St. Louis, the afternoon taping of a local talk show completed, and a few hours to kill before the thing was aired. Kareem only handles the publicity for my eastern tours — where the big action is — but out in the hinterlands most book-pushers are on their own, trudging from airports to taxis, to and from studios, bookstores or wherever the powers-that-be have decreed. Real glamorous stuff, that. Especially when some dink fails to pick you up in a rainstorm or the show's host thinks your name is more inspiring than your book.

So, what to do. I could go out and see Charlie

Smythe. I'd talked to him a couple weeks back on the phone, and promised to stop by and see an E-type Jaguar roadster he'd taken in on a Rolls. Said it was pristine, which it would have to be if he so described it. That sounded like a real fun way to pass the time, so instead, I visited Lydia Arbaugh.

Like I said earlier, I really hadn't planned to ever see or contact Lydia again. That's why I kept her name, address and phone number in my billfold. "Yeah, I suppose that woman never crosses your mind anymore — that's why you keep her precious name and phone number in your wallet next to your heart." "I carry my billfold in my back pants pocket." "See!"

Oh, the seedier side of marriage — something to consider if ever I decide to take the nesting plunge again ..."

I dialed Lydia's number several times. No answer. So I hired a cab, and headed to her house. Normally, I wouldn't take the chance of finding someone at home after getting no answer on the phone, and for that matter, it's not my custom to arrive at anyone's office or residence unannounced, but Lydia's address was only a few blocks from Charlie's establishment, so I justified the trip with all that logic I just layed on you.

I was really quite surprised when the doorbell brought a quick response, and even more surprised to see Lydia open the door. But the real surprise prize goes to Lydia — she appeared to be in total shock, lacking all her usual and abundant poise.

"Why ... why ... D-Derek. Derek Dax." She alternately stammered and shouted.

"In the flesh, madam. I just happened to be in the neighborhood ..." Geez, doesn't anybody appreciate a bad pun anymore? Lydia didn't, and remained so speechless and ill at ease, my desire was to return to my cab, take off and try to pretend like I'd never made this apparent blunder. Instead, I went to the curb and over-tipped the cabbie.

"Come in, Derek. Come in. You just startled me so. I am so surprised to ..."

"See me. Yeah, well, as I said, I just thought since I was in your fair city, anyway ... I should have called first. In fact, I did dial your number a few times, but no answer."

"Yes ... we ... Daniel and I ... just got home."

"Oh, good. I'd like to meet your son, Lydia. Is he around now?"

"No ... no ... he's down the street playing with friends. What is the matter with me, Derek — my manners — do sit down. Would you care for a beer?"

"Beer? No, no thanks. I never acquired a taste for the stuff."

"Wine then. I've got some burgundy and some white, I think."

"The red's fine. Are you okay, Lydia? You seem distraught."

"Oh no, I'm fine. I'll be right back with the drinks."

When she'd left the room, I looked around and couldn't help but observe the shabby disorderliness of the surroundings. Grimy furniture, soiled carpeting, ash trays filled with cigarette butts. The whole place was totally out of character for the Lydia I'd known, and yes, even loved a little, back at the house that Dax built. Weird. I was wishing very strongly that I'd left the memory alone, and was sitting in Charlie's sable brown Jag right now, when Lydia returned, drinks in hand.

"So, what brings you to Saint Louie, Louie?" Bright, breezy — recovering, but over-compensating.

"Oh, I did the Ronson show this afternoon. It'll be aired tonight if you get a change to see it."

"Oh yes, I'll be sure to tune it in."

I wondered how, since the set in the corner of the room had its eye punched out. "Lydia, I ... uh" my thoughts drifted as I noticed her once lustrous, meticulously manicured fingernails were not only gone, but cut or chewed to the quick. She noticed me staring at her hands, and self consciously disappeared her fingers into little fists.

"I've been working in the flower garden. My nails are a mess — I'm a mess, Derek — I hate to have you see me this way."

For my mental file I recorded the horrible, sick,

disjointed feeling that had now totally enveloped my mind and body. Upon retrieval, when it came time to set these words to paper, the sensation had not abated. It was like one time in your wild impetuous youth, you ordered three dozen roses, tediously removed all the petals, and used them to cover your nuptial bed. Your bride was stunningly nubile, the champagne chilled and fizzy, and your blushing bride became a nymphomaniac.

Ten years later, to commemorate the momentous occasion, you lovingly set everything into motion to ensure recreation of that propitious event. But somehow, despite your vivid memory, your diligence and your anticipation, the repeat performance ultimately comes off more like dandelion greens, stale beer, your wife's in hair curlers and has the curse.

I snapped out of my funk and said, "Did you ever find out what Paul did with the car?"

"No, I never could figure that out."

"Well, you won't believe what ..."

"Oh, excuse me, I didn't know you had company, Lydia." The husky voice was followed by a man of about forty-five, full beard, faded red tank top and a pair of those God-awful blue jean cut-offs that I have often offered to sign a petition to ban, if someone would draft one. No man should wear shorts. Most women should not wear revealing clothes. Only cute little boys and girls, and cute big girls.

"Uh ... Derek Dax ... this is my ... friend ... Alan Wilson."

"Alan Wilson? There's a coincidence. One of my old school chums is named Alan Wilson. He's a doctor. You met him at the class reunion, Lydia ..."

There was a clammy silence. Neither Lydia or the hairy lump seemed disposed to small talk, and I sure as hell wasn't in the mood. All I wanted to do was get away from this mistake and expunge it from my recall.

"Well, listen, folks, I appreciate the hospitality, but I've an appointment downtown, so I'd best be getting on."

There was an awkward exchange of good-byes, and I found myself on the front walk without transportation. I'd forgotten I'd arrived by taxi, let alone the fact I'd dismissed him after discovering Lydia was in residence. Well, I certainly wasn't going back and ask to use the phone. I strolled down the street. It was a pleasant neighborhood of fifteen thousand dollar houses — if you'd bought one when they were built post WWII. Now, they'd fetch about fifty thou apiece. I was mentally figuring out the cost for construction materials for one of those cracker boxes — home construction is on a par with old cars in my hobbies department — when I ran into two little boys.

Actually, they ran into me. First, a little freckled-faced red head, followed on his heels by a touseled brown-haired little fellow, whom I immediately recognized, as a miniature of his father, Robert Lamphere. "Hello there, guys. Hey — you're Daniel Arbaugh, aren't you?"

The boy looked at me suspiciously, tossing a football back and forth from hand to hand. "I don't know you, mister."

"No, you're right. But I know your mother and your dad."

"You know my dad? He's dead, you know ..." His head hung down for a moment, more like he was ashamed than sad.

"Yes, Daniel, I know. I'm sorry. Your father was a fine, very smart man. We went to school together. Used to play together just like you and your friend here."

"I'm going home, now. Would you like to come with me? My mom's there. You said you know her."

"Yes. Well, I just came from there, Daniel. And I've got to be going. But listen, I'll be on television tonight — maybe your mother will let you see the show."

"Teevee's busted. He kicked it the other night." His dejection was mixed with anger.

"Who broke the teevee? Mr. Wilson?"

"Who? No ... Uncle Justin. He kicked it."

It's never happened to me, and I hope it never does, but if Kareem ever elects to make me the recipient of his infamous 'Pakistani Parachutist

Karate' maneuver, I already know the total
devastation it wreaks. I experienced it when that
little boy said, 'Uncle Justin.' It all came back in a
sickening flash. The intricate too-impossible-not-
to-be-true tale of intrigue, quasi-rape, accidental
murder, body disposal, et. al.

My mouth went dry and my heart pounded, and I
probably stood with my mouth agape, because the
freckled face said, "Are you all right, mister? You
having a heart attack or somethin'?"

"No, not yet ... well, Daniel, nice to meet you.
Goodbye."

I hurried away, and four blocks down the street
hailed a cab and headed for Charlie's place. I sat in
the Jag, had some dinner with Charlie, haggled over
the price he wanted for the sportscar, bought it
anyway (he refused to budge from the fourteen
grand figure — even though I bought him a fabulous
steak dinner!) and took the Jag out for a drive. To
Lydia's street.

As I approached the house I mentally slapped
my face to remind myself of one of Kareem's basic
tenets; Don't walk into a potentially dangerous
situation if you can creep. I pushed the twelve
cylinders past the house, and glided to a stop around
the first corner.

I got out, locked the doors, had second thoughts,
unlocked the doors, and for good measure rolled
down the windows. No use inviting someone to

slash the canvas top to gain entrance. If it was stolen, perhaps if I ever got it back, it would at least be more or less intact.

There was only one street light between the corner and Lydia's house. I walked slowly but deliberately down the street towards her house, but turned into a yard two houses away and purposefully walked to the rear yard, like I lived there. No one was around to challenge me, so I made a ninety degree towards Lydia's backyard, and when I got there hurdled a waist-high fence and landed quietly in a spot, some thirty feet from her garage.

I was attracted to a light and some voices coming from within. The windows were all covered over, but I found a pinhole size opening in the paper covering one of them, and by sticking my eyeball against it could see inside very clearly. Lydia and 'Alan Wilson.' A red Subaru wagon, a similar model to the mustard one Kareem and I'd deep-sixed. This one had its hood removed, and it was leaning against a wall. Lydia was leaning against it, and the hairy one was puzzling over the engine compartment.

"I don't understand it, Justin — we've done everything just like Paul and you did the first time. Why won't it work?"

"I told you, dammit. He designed that special set of bevel gears for the friction reduction system on his own. I never really even looked at it that close.

Besides, that's not my field, I'm the electronic wizard, remember?"

"If only you hadn't antagonized Paul so much ...'

"Me? Shit, woman — you're the one that kept pushing him to sell the thing — all that big money — all the fancy, high-falutin' things you wanted .. Hell, you all but drove him crazy!"

"Your purposely picking that big fight with him — telling him you and I were screwing each other behind his back — that didn't help matters any, you jerk."

At that, he walked over and back-handed her across the face. His manner and her reaction told me that it was a fairly common way they had of ending a conversation. But then she paced the short distance to where he was now bent over the engine compartment, with his back to her. She pressed her body to his hunched form, and slipped her hand into his cutoffs and started to massage his ...

"Son of a bitch!" The minute I'd allowed that exclamation to escape, I realized I'd goofed, but the humor of the remark struck me, as well, for indeed, a little son of a bitch was relentlessly biting at my right leg. The nasty little beast looked like a cross between an English bulldog and an alligator, and he clung tenaciously to my calf. The pain, plus the instinct to run were superceded by the realization that I wasn't going anywhere, nor was there going to be any relief from that stabbing pain until I eliminated the cause.

I let out a great "Arggh!" and willed my body's full power to my right fist, exactly as I'd been taught by Kareem. The blow literally smashed the animal's head, and he was probably dead before his teeth freed my flesh.

All this ruckus evidently had caused massageus interruptus, because Lydia and Justin were now outside, observing the spectacle.

"Howdy, folks — just happened to be in the neighborhood, again. Jesus, does that leg *hurt!*"

Justin was wielding a pry bar of considerable stature, so his timely suggestion that I come join them in the garage was met by a hesitant but limping reply.

Inside, I didn't wait for an invitation to sit down, and plopped on a wooden stool next to the car.

"I told you he knew when the kid came home, dammit!"

"Derek, why did you come here this afternoon?"

"Misplaced affection. Stupid curiosity. Who knows? What difference does it make?" As I spoke I squeezed the wound on my leg hard, trying to make it bleed to hopefully remove all the little raby babies that were probably swimming towards a new home in my brain. The pain was excruciating, and I feared that I might faint. Humor. Be light. Witty. Take your mind off the pain. Mind control. Hell, Kareem literally would not even bleed under these circumstances. I've seen him actually stop blood flow in a wound of his own with nothing but sheer willpower.

"So, folks — you can't make it work, eh? It's just as well. Paul had the right idea. Forget it before you get in Dutch with the wrong people."

"You're already in Dutch with the wrong people, Dax."

"Oh, contraire, mon ami. Lydia here and I are lovers, didn't you know? Oh yes, back at my big plush, hedonistic estate, we had a great old time, just screwed ourself blue. You should try it sometime..." It had the desired effect. The poor jealous ass came close to me, raised the bar high, and gave out the most agonizing blood-curdling scream you could imagine as I grabbed his goodies and rang his chimes.

As he writhed about me on the floor, I reached down and picked up the pry bar he'd dropped, although he would not be of further threat for awhile. Lydia would be however, as she now stood quietly, with her eyes trained on me as well as a small pistol. "Sit down, Derek!" Her once sensual, soft brown eyes looked hard and mean.

I sat down, as much from pain as from disgust. "Okay, girl. Ya got me. The jig's up. What now, you kill me, I suppose? No? You hadn't really thought that out yet, had you ... Well listen, let me help you. You could bury my body somewhere out in the

country — just like Paul did with this zombie here."
I looked at Justin. He was in very bad shape, near
unconsciousness.

"Why did you have to come here! We were so
close! We might have been rich! You spoiled it
all ...!"

By God, Kareem was right. The eyes do flinch
just a tad before the trigger finger squeezes off. I
jerked my body to the left, instinctively not wanting
to land on my injured right leg. The single shot
intended for me caught Justin above the right ear,
and his writhing from the earlier injury stopped.

Lydia, realizing what she'd done, shook convul-
sively and raised her hands to claw her own face, a
wild impetuous gesture resulting in accidental
suicide, because the gun discharged and removed
her left temple.

I felt no compulsion to go to her. She was dead to
me now, completely.

I sat there for quite awhile, thinking. Mostly, I
just wanted to smoke, but I couldn't risk the odor of
pipe smoke considering what I'd decided to do.
Slowly, I dragged myself to my feet. The pain
caused a wave of nausea, but I willed my dinner to
stay put — I had enough to clean up as it was.

The pain became bearable after the injured leg
grew accustomed to the weight of my body, and I
walked around the garage a little just to make
certain that I had a chance to physically complete

my mission. I shut the garage light off, opened the door slowly and looked outside. No one was around, and most house lights in the neighborhood were out, with the exception of Lydia's where it appeared that a kitchen light had been left on. I walked quietly to the door leading to the house. It was unlocked, and I reached in and snapped off the switch.

No one stirred, so I walked as briskly as I could to the front walk, and down the street. I was grateful to see the Jaguar still there. Wasn't even stripped. Chrome wire wheels glistened, anxious to start spinning. I got in with a great deal of discomfort and had to use both hands to lift the bad leg over the sill.

I didn't think I'd be able to exert any pressure on the accelerator, and since the Jag was a four speed I had to use my good leg for the clutch. Fortunately, the idle was set too fast, and I was able to creep the machine into motion, the hum of the engine just nudging the silence of the night. I finally got the car into the vacant stall next to the Subaru, and closed the door.

Some peculiar inner desire made me go look at the bodies. Why? To see if they were still there? Still dead? I don't know, but thereafter I began my frantic, nearly impossible assignment of removing the basic components of the electric apparatus in the car. My main objective was to obfuscate the principal evidence of the car's uniqueness. Anyone might build a regular battery-powered car, so it was the generator and linkage apparatus that most concerned me. I crawled over, under and through the little car, wrenching out the bolts and putting the smaller pieces of machinery in the Jag.

The generator itself was the biggest challenge. I rigged up a block and tackle to the only available overhead fastener — a steel track from the sectional door, and amidst much muttering and cussing, plus a real fear that the track would give way under the weight, got the generator free of the Subaru's cargo area, and swung it into the trunk of the Jaguar.

I then tidied up the place, made the scene look as normally abnormal as possible, and tied the open deck lid down over the generator. I looked one last time at Lydia and said soundlessly, "Good-bye, Lydia. You sure were a lady. Once."

I got the Jag out, shut the lights off and closed the door. I was in the car and ready to go when I realized my error, and had to painfully get back out, go to the garage and turn the lights back on. At the very last moment I remembered something else. I went to the rear of the garage, outside, and found the carcass of the dog and threw it into the open trunk next to the generator.

Once I got the car onto the street, I mustered up my resolve and trounced the accelerator down hard, and got the hell away from there. I drove several blocks, stopped at a pay phone and called the police. I used a heavily disguised southern accent to report "some strange goin's on — possibly a shot or two, but maybe it weren't. Mightabeen a car backfirin'." I gave the address, and told them, "I think there's a child in the house — a little girl, I think — might be alone. Better check on that, too." I probably went overboard on the subterfuge, but it crossed my mind that given some of the crazy coincidences of late, if I simply called up the police and gave them the straight facts in my own voice, right about then the desk sergeant would probably have his set tuned into the local show which I'd taped earlier.

The next couple hours were devoted to further polluting the Mississippi with parts of the car, getting myself cleaned up a little, and then a visit to the emergency ward. I must have looked really weird dragging myself and that bloody furry glob up the hall. I gave a fictitious name, told the receptionist I was a transient that had been victimized by the nasty little creature I'd brought with me, and after treatment spent twenty-four miserable hours waiting for the lab report on the dog. Negative. No rabies. My brain would remain at its normal muddled self.

At Lambert airport I bought a copy of the *Dispatch,* and after a search found a one paragraph account of one of the city's most recent tragedies, headlined, *"Domestic Murder/Suicide."* Nothing in the brief report eluded to anything unusual. Just a thirty year old woman who decided to terminate her housekeeping arrangement with her middle-aged roomie.

From St. Louis I flew back home for a few days before heading back on the promo tour. Charlie arranged to have the Jaguar shipped to McLean. Kareem joined me for a few hours during the stay, and found me at the cottage one afternoon mulling over the whole bizarre affair. The St. Louis post script didn't seem to come as any shock to him. "Mrs. Arbaugh's eyes seemed warm only to you, Mr. Dax. To everyone else they were deadly cold and calculating. I don't know her relationship with Mr. Arbaugh, but I think maybe he's fortunate to be starting a new life now."

"You really do believe in that part of your upbringing — about reincarnation, I mean — despite all the other teachings of Islam and Hinduism you've disavowed?"

Kareem walked to the cottage door, flung it open and swept his arms magnanimously over the peaceful meadow and woods beyond. "How could all of this have been created for just one lifetime?"

I looked thoughtfully at my complicated companion and replied, "How could it, indeed."

Epilogue

When recording the events of this particular adventure, I hesitated hard and long before adding what I came to refer to as 'the postscript' — that segment that took place after Kareem and I had laid the mustard colored Subaru to rest.

Everyone loves a story of intrigue, romance, high idealism and unrequited love. It would thus have been easy and convenient to tag chapter twelve with '-30-', the writer's signal to typesetters that 'no more copy follows.'

As I say, that would have been simple, but not honest. And I've never lied or held back on you yet — so why start now? Life isn't always as pleasant as we'd like it to be, and now and again that reality must be faced. Sure, Lydia Arbaugh was everything wonderous as I described her to be early-on, but she was also, after all, a human being subject to avarice, passion, misdirected loyalties and all other trenchant failings of the species. But she's gone now. 'Speak kindly of the dead.' So be it.

On the bright side: We got Carlita Phillips as a permament member of our household, and although it's too early to disclose any facts, my lawyers have been making discreet inquiries into the possibility of one Daniel David Lamphere eventually having his residence and last name changed one more time. Daniel David Dax would have a rather rhythmic flow to the sound, eh wot?

Now then, here's your
-30-

Dean F. V. Du Vall until recently was best known for his prolific output of financial writings in such fields as stocks, commodities and real estate, and has published some three dozen books, manuals, courses and cassette tape programs of a financial / technical nature.

But with the advent of his first novel, "The Big Dream" (published by Lyle Stuart, Inc., New York) Du Vall discovered a fresh love, writing fiction. Soon he created a whole new series character, Derek Dax, who has been described as a a much needed hero figure for today's society which too often perhaps, is presently only with anti-hero figures.

Dax, while not exactly a bumbler, doesn't pretend to be perfect and frequently his sidekick, the bigger-than-life Pakistani, Kareem Khan, is allowed to outshine his "boss."

The first book in the Derek Dax series, "The Enchanted Cottage," took observers by storm as it was strongly suggested that Du Vall's penchant for personal marketing (through direct mail) would never work with fiction as it does with higher priced non-fiction works.

But Du Vall devotees and friends rallied to spread the word about his exciting new venture, the Derek Dax series, and now with "Class Prophecy: Murder," the second book in the series, Du Vall and Dax are well on their merry way to becoming household words. Motion picture rights to the first two books have been sold and there is a growing cult of Dax readers eagerly awaiting each new book in the series. And there will be more as Du Vall now devotes nearly all his time and energy to the project.

A PERSONAL MESSAGE ...

In the back of "The Enchanted Cottage" I asked you to do me a favor if you liked the book; to tell all your friends!

And that must surely have happened, because we've been hearing from people all over the world, so if you were one of those who has assisted me in spreading the Dax-word, my sincere thanks.

As you read this, I'm in a secluded northwoods cabin pounding out another Derek Dax adventure — and the predicaments, problems and dangers I'm giving the poor chap are so nasty that I'd best reward his with some nice romantic interludes, eh wot?(!)

But my mail is forwarded here, so as another Dean (Martin) used to say, "Please keep those cards 'n letters coming!" I welcome your thoughts and suggestions — good or bad!

Dean F. V. Du Vall

P.S. If you got the copy of "ClassProphecy: Murder" from a store or as a gift, be sure to send me your name and address and I'll personally let you know as soon as the next book in the series is released. But don't worry if you've ordered either of the Derek Dax books directly from us — you're already on the list!

IF YOU MISSED ...

... the very *first* book in the exciting Derek Dax series — then you've also missed some of the finest unadulterated action available on the adventure/mystery/romance scene.

"The Enchanted Cottage" is where it all started; while on an east coast book promotional tour Dax meets the principals and recurring characters of the series (including the incomparable Kareem Khan), and together they solve their very first murder mystery. But Dax, recently widowered following a tragic air disaster is highly vulnerable on a personal level and susceptible to the sophisticated charms of an intriguing English lady with questionable motives. Get filled in on the background details that led to the current episode by reading "The Enchanted Cottage."

If your local bookseller is out of stock you may order directly from the publisher.

 DAX ACTION BOOKS
Division of Du Vall Press
Financial Publications
920 West Grand River
Williamston, Michigan 48895

NOTE: Avoid writer's cramp! simply address your order to:
DAX 14-EC, Williamston, MI 48895

Please rush the following:

☐ Class Prophecy: Murder @ $6.95 ea.
☐ The Enchanted Cottage @ $6.95 ea.
☐ The Big Dream (hardcover) @ $10.00 ea.

Total enclosed: _____
(payable in U.S. funds)

—All prices INCLUDE shipping/handling—

☐ Check   ☐ Money Order   ☐ **VISA**   ☐ master charge

_____

_____

_____ Zip _____

Card No.
☐☐☐☐ ☐☐☐☐ ☐☐☐☐ ☐☐☐☐
Interbank No. ____ Mo. Yr.____
Expiration Date

A catalog of Mr. Du Vall's books will be included with each order or may be ordered separately for $2.00.

FOR THE COLLECTOR/INVESTOR: Each of the Derek Dax books is now available in a special limited first edition, hardbound in genuine burgundy leather with gold leaf imprint. Numbered, dated and personally signed by author. $100.00 each. A great and timeless gift for a very special friend or for ... yourself. (Because you're worth it!) Please specify title(s).

IF YOU MISSED ...

... the very *first* book in the exciting Derek Dax series — then you've also missed some of the finest unadulterated action available on the adventure/mystery/romance scene.

"The Enchanted Cottage" is where it all started; while on an east coast book promotional tour Dax meets the principals and recurring characters of the series (including the incomparable Kareem Khan), and together they solve their very first murder mystery. But Dax, recently widowered following a tragic air disaster is highly vulnerable on a personal level and susceptible to the sophisticated charms of an intriguing English lady with questionable motives. Get filled in on the background details that led to the current episode by reading "The Enchanted Cottage."

If your local bookseller is out of stock you may order directly from the publisher.

 DAX ACTION BOOKS
Division of Du Vall Press
Financial Publications
920 West Grand River
Williamston, Michigan 48895

> *NOTE: Avoid writer's cramp! simply address your order to:*
> **DAX 14-EC, Williamston, MI 48895**

Please rush the following:

☐ Class Prophecy: Murder @ $6.95 ea.
☐ The Enchanted Cottage @ $6.95 ea.
☐ The Big Dream (hardcover) @ $10.00 ea.

Total enclosed: _____
(payable in U.S. funds)

—All prices INCLUDE shipping/handling—

☐ Check   ☐ Money Order   ☐ VISA BankAmericard®   ☐ master charge

_____

_____

_____ Zip _____

Card No.

☐☐☐☐ ☐☐☐☐ ☐☐☐☐ ☐☐☐☐
|____|Interbank No. ____Mo. Yr.____
Expiration Date

A catalog of Mr. Du Vall's books will be included with each order or may be ordered separately for $2.00.

FOR THE COLLECTOR/INVESTOR: Each of the Derek Dax books is now available in a special limited first edition, hardbound in genuine burgundy leather with gold leaf imprint. Numbered, dated and personally signed by author. $100.00 each. A great and timeless gift for a very special friend or for ... yourself. (Because you're worth it!) Please specify title(s).